# NEW RIVER BREEZE

### BY
## ED ROBINSON

This is dedicated to those that hike, climb, kayak, canoe, camp, and fish in the wilds of northwest North Carolina.

# THE NEW RIVER

Many claim that the New River is the second oldest river in the world, after the Nile. Not many rivers can lay claim to the fact that they are older than the mountains wherein their course lies. Most rivers that have their beginnings in the mountains, slide off their crest, and then follow at the base of the mountains. That is not true with the New. Its two forks converge in North Carolina and then continue to stay within the crest of the Appalachians throughout the river's duration; basically eroding and cutting through the middle of the mountains as they rose up.

Many scientists believe that when the Appalachian Mountains were formed, the New River simply rose up with the mountains, and that is why it remains in the crest. Scientists also believe the Appalachian Mountains to be the oldest mountains in the world. It is possible that the New River is older than any mountain range in the world. Finally, the New River's mountain contorting course has exposed rocks that are over one billion years old.

(Source-National Park Service)

# ONE

The last thing I expected to see on a camping trip was a naked guy running through the woods. I looked at Brody with a shrug, and she confirmed that we had indeed seen a bare-assed lunatic running and rambling in some unintelligible language. Though my curiosity was naturally aroused, I had no desire to chase after him. Instead, we chose to figure out which campsite he had come from.

We were on the New River, at a camping area that could only be reached by canoe or kayak. We had to carry in everything that we thought we needed to survive for a few days in the woods. I'd been laid up with bad knees long enough to miss being out in nature. They were much better now, but I figured paddling a canoe was a safe enough exercise. All I wanted to do was build a little campfire and look up at the stars.

We walked along the river, looking for other campers. On the way, we collected articles of clothing strewn about. We saw assorted items floating down the river too. We even came upon a canoe stuck in the rocks at a bend in the river. It was an easy trail to follow, and it led us to a sorry sight. A young woman was sitting on a log crying. She was surrounded by the remnants of a campsite. The tent was shredded. An empty cooler was lodged up in a tree. Food had been dumped from containers and strewn about. I let Brody handle approaching the woman.

"What's your name?" Brody asked.

"Jessie Lynn," she replied. "Jessie Lynn Naylor."

"Are you hurt?"

"Just my pride," she said. "He's gone plum crazy."

"Are you sure he didn't hurt you?"

"He wasn't concerned about me," she said. "But he sure was mad at our stuff."

"What happened?" Brody asked. "What set him off?"

"He took some of them magic mushrooms," Jessie said. "He was happy at first; then he got real weird."

I listened with interest. I'd eaten mushrooms in my youth, several times. Not once did I get the urge to run naked through the forest. Mostly it had been a pleasant experience. On the other hand, I'd also dropped acid a few times when I was young and dumb. That stuff could make you do some crazy things. My most memorable experience was thinking that I was in attendance at the second coming of Jesus. As it turned out, I was at a Stones' concert. The old JFK Stadium looked a lot like the Roman Coliseum to me, and all the people flocking to it were Christian worshippers. Thankfully, my friends steered me along and kept me out of trouble until we were safely inside.

I suspected that the naked runner had taken more than mushrooms. He might not come down for many hours. The girl didn't have a usable tent or much left to eat. She needed help. I asked her what she wanted to do, and she said she would have to wait for her boyfriend to come back. She couldn't leave him alone out there. Brody suggested that I could find him and bring him in, but I refused.

"This is supposed to be a little vacation for us," I said. "I was hoping for a little 'one with the wilderness experience,' not to wrestle a dude with his dick swinging in the wind."

"You want her to come to our tent?" Brody asked.

I did not want her to come to our tent. We rarely had visitors to our cabin. Sharing a tent with a total stranger with a deranged boyfriend on the loose was not my idea of a vacation. I knew that to please Brody I'd have to help the girl, but I was struggling to come up with some alternative method of helping. Just when I thought all was lost, another couple emerged from the trees.

"Hope it wasn't a bear attack," the man said.

"Boyfriend having a bad trip," I said. "I'm Breeze, this is Brody, and this young lady here is Jessie Lynn."

"I'm Linwood," he said. "This is my wife Betty, but in the woods, we go by Loon and Chickadee."

"We were unaware that we needed woods names," I said. "We're just Breeze and Brody."

"Bring your booze over to our campfire tonight, and we'll decide on wilderness nicknames for you," he said. "Now, what can we do for you, Jessie Lynn?"

"I've got no place to sleep," she said. "But I don't want to intrude on any of you."

"You don't have sleeping bags?" Linwood asked.

"Bobby threw them in the river," she said. "They floated off that way."

"We saw a canoe back in that direction," I said. "Is that yours?"

"Probably," she said. "But I can't get to it."

"Brody and I will try to get the canoe, and we'll look for sleeping bags," I said. "Maybe Loon and Chickadee here can help patch up that tent; at least enough to get you through the night. We'll all meet back here and fix some chow. We can swap lies over the fire while we wait for your boyfriend."

"I can't pay you nothing," she said. "But I sure do appreciate the help."

"We all help one another out here," Linwood said. "It's the 'code of the woods'."

I didn't know much about any code of the woods, but offering a hand when it was needed was just being a good human being. If we could set up Jessie to make it until her boyfriend showed up, that was good enough for me, as long as she didn't have to sleep with us. Brody and I returned to our camp and launched our canoe. I would have rather had a kayak, but they offered no room to carry supplies. Besides, the river was no deeper than two feet for most of its length. If we capsized the thing, we wouldn't drown.

We paddled back to where we'd seen the canoe, picking up a soggy sleeping bag on the way. For Jessie's sake, I hoped the synthetic materials would dry quickly. Before heading back to her site, we gathered up some food for dinner and a bottle of Old Smokey Tennessee Whiskey that I'd brought for medicinal purposes. You never know when you might suffer from a rattlesnake bite. I was willing to sacrifice it for social purposes instead.

There was no sign of the naked boyfriend when we returned to Jessie's site. The Loon and Chickadee had salvaged enough tent material to make a two-sided structure for her to sleep under. I hung the sleeping bag up in the trees and made sure it was draining well. Brody brought some dead wood and twigs to start a fire under it. Jessie herself wasn't much help. She seemed to be in a state of shock.

"You sober?" I asked. "Because you need to get your shit together."

"I didn't eat no mushrooms," she said. "Just wondering how I find myself out here with nothing is all."

"This ain't no picnic," I told her. "No help is coming other than what you've already got. You're lucky that there are folks here willing to pitch in."

"You're right," she said. "I've got to stop feeling sorry for myself."

"You'll be fine," Brody said. "Help me gather up some more wood."

Brody and Jessie went off on a wood gathering mission. Chickadee worried over cleaning up the trash from Bobby's rampage. I got a minute alone with the Loon.

"You armed?" I asked quietly.

"Hunting knife," he said. "You?"

"Forty cal," I said. "Plus a knife. Brody's carrying too."

"You think this guy will be trouble?"

"More likely he's lost," I said. "Cold and scared out there somewhere."

"Should we search for him?"

"I'd let him come down first," I suggested. "He'll be easier to handle. He might even find his way back here on his own. Who knows?"

"How much do you know about this area?" he asked. "We're not from around here. Came down from Maine to check it out."

"I'm not schooled on this part of the state specifically," I said. "But I'm damn good in the woods. I've been exploring these mountains for a while now. Do some tracking for the police from time to time."

"No kidding?" he said. "So, you're an experienced mountain man."

"Not like Jeremiah Johnson or anything," I said. "But I know my way around."

"I'm a trail guide back in Maine," he said. "The terrain isn't that much different here. I reckon I could be useful if we've got to go rescue this knucklehead."

"Good to know," I said. "But let's worry about that in the morning. I brought a little octane to add spark to the fireside conversation."

"As did I, my friend," he said. "Great minds think alike."

We got the area cleaned up and secured Jessie's shelter. Her sleeping bag was still damp, but it seemed to be drying quickly hanging by the fire. Brody made a bigger fire in the designated fire pit which we used to cook hotdogs and fend off the evening chill. When I got a chance, I warned Brody to stay alert for the return of mushroom man.

"Keep your wits," I whispered. "Trippers are unpredictable."

"I'm alert," she said. "Don't worry about me, just take it easy on that whiskey."

"Understood," I said. "But we can't stay with her all night."

"Let me talk to her," she said. "See if there's anything to worry about."

I sat next to the Loon and produced my bottle. He showed me his, which was Allen's Coffee Flavored Brandy. I'd never heard of it but was willing to give it a try. It wasn't as smooth as Tennessee Whiskey, but it left a nice warm feeling after it went down.

"Fireball is all the rage these days up in Maine," he said. "But I'll stick with the tried and true."

"We're too close to Tennessee to drink that stuff," I said. "Give this a sip. Nice and easy."

"That is nice," he said. "Smooth as all get out."

"Smooth as Tennessee Whiskey," I said.

"Sweet as Strawberry Wine," he replied.

"Warm as a glass of brandy."

"And honey, I stay stoned on your love all the time," he finished.

"Please, Breeze," Brody said. "Don't start singing."

The Loon was a good storyteller, and he had a bunch of them from his trail days in Maine. He dominated our fireside chat, which was fine by me. I reclined back against a log and looked up at the stars. I also kept my ears open for any sound of movement in the dark woods around us. Brody mostly stood; adding logs to the fire and checking on the dryness of Jessie Lynn's sleeping bag. Chickadee sat with the poor girl, which seemed to comfort her. The couple from Maine felt at ease in the woods, unlike Jessie. I took an occasional half sip from a bottle but stayed sober. The Loon took healthier slugs, but it didn't seem to bother him. I noticed him scanning the trees from time to time, just like Brody was doing.

Eventually, the warmth of the fire and the warmth of the whiskey conspired to put me to sleep. I yawned and motioned to Brody that we should be leaving.

"Are you going to okay here tonight?" Brody asked Jessie.

"He won't hurt me," she replied. "I'm more worried about him out there in the dark with no clothes on."

"We'll be close by," The Loon said. "Just holler if you need help."

"You all go ahead," Jessie said. "I've taken up enough of your time today. Thanks for everything."

"Seriously, girl," Brody said. "Yell if you're in trouble. We'll be here in a flash."

I took down the sleeping bag and carried it to what was left of her tent. It was almost dry. The fire was contained in a pit, so we decided to let it burn itself out. Maybe it would provide heat long enough for Jessie to fall asleep. We all pitied her, but we'd done all that we could. It was time to turn in. The Loon pulled me aside before we departed.

"If that fool doesn't show up we'll have to search for him," he said.

"Get some rest," I said. "Tomorrow could be a long day."

"Thanks for the whiskey," he said.

"Thanks for the brandy," I said. "It's been nice meeting you."

We pulled the canoes further from the river's edge and started walking back to our camp. I pulled my pistol from the back of my pants and carried it in my hand. We were soon in near total darkness. The woods took on a spooky feeling. I made Brody stop and stay still so I could listen. I heard nothing alarming, so we continued. Our campsite was undisturbed.

I lit a lantern so I could see well enough to build our own fire. I absentmindedly tucked the gun in the front of my pants while I worked. When I crawled into the tent to snuggle with Brody, it pushed up against her.

"Is that a gun in your pocket, or are you just happy to see me?"

"Shit, sorry," I said, placing the weapon to the side. "Now, where were we?"

"I think you were about to demonstrate that today's distractions won't affect the performance of your duties."

"Only one way to find out," I said.

I fulfilled my half of the bargain admirably, but sleep overcame me in a hurry soon after. There was no post-coital cuddling that night. There were no interruptions to our sleep either. If the naked man had found his way back, he was awfully quiet about it. I crawled out of the tent and fumbled with our newly purchased percolator. I restarted the fire and wedged the pot on some rocks to heat up. I wasn't fully awake yet, so I reached for the pot to pour a cup and burned the crap out of my hand. I made enough painful sounds to wake Brody.

"Smooth move, Sherlock," she said. "Go dunk your hand in the river. I'll pour."

The water temperature was still cool enough to do me some good. I'd been quick pulling away from the heat so I didn't think it would blister. My hand was red and tender, though. I'd been reaching for a coffee pot the first thing every morning for over thirty years. It was a reflex. The need for caffeine overrode my good sense not to grab a hot pot out of a fire. Brody came down and set a cup of coffee on the ground beside me.

"Use your good hand," she said. "Keep the other one in the water."

"I guess we should check on Jessie Lynn," I said. "Offer her some breakfast or something."

"Stay here," she said. "I'll go look in on her. If she wants, I'll bring her back."

"Is there enough for another cup?"

"Half, maybe," she said. "I left a dish towel to pick it up with."

The hand didn't hurt that bad. My pride was in worse shape. Some mountain man I was. I was able to pour the rest of the coffee without further damage. I pushed the rocks around with a stick so they could accommodate a frying pan. We'd brought bacon and fake eggs that came in a cardboard container. We only planned to stay for a few days, and really couldn't afford to share too much of our food. We could always call it quits and go home where the coffee pot didn't bite.

The bacon was cooked, and I was starting the eggs when Brody returned alone.

"The Loon and Chickadee are feeding her at their place," she said. "No sign of the boyfriend."

"You realize we're going to have to go look for him," I said.

"You just so happen to have some skills in that area," she said. "An unexpected adventure."

"Not one that I signed up for."

"It will do you good," she suggested. "Out in the wilderness, doing your thing."

"A naked dumbass shouldn't be hard to find," I said. "He's sobered up by now, wondering how he got wherever he is."

"Why do people take drugs that make them crazy?"

"Mushrooms are relatively harmless," I said. "He got into something else."

"Personal experience?"

"I tried them a few times," I said. "A long time ago in a place far away."

"What did they do to you?"

"Some euphoria, happy feelings, seeing trails with any movement," I said. "Felt organic with no hangover later. Of all the stupid shit I did back then, that was the safest."

"Would you do it again?"

"It's been a long time," I said. "But I think that under the right circumstances, I would try it."

"What would those circumstances be?"

"Controlled environment with someone you trust," I said. "Like at home with you."

"I will file that away for future reference," she said. "I've never done anything like that."

"I wasn't a straight arrow hoping to be an FBI agent someday," I said. "I went through a phase where I would try just about anything, except needles."

"So what do you think happened to this guy?"

"Somebody put regular mushrooms in a bag and dropped some acid on them."

"People are strange," she said.

"Now he'll be exhausted, thirsty, and confused," I said. "He hasn't eaten, and he has no clothes. Doesn't know where he is or how he got there. He's in trouble."

"Eat up," she said. "We'll round up the troops and save his sorry ass."

We cleaned up our breakfast mess and prepared a light pack for the day. We spread out on the way to Jessie's and looked for Bobbie's clothes. Brody found a pair of jeans, but that was it. We found the girl with the Maine couple at their site.

"Is everyone ready for a little hiking today?" I asked.

"We've got to find Bobbie," Jessie said. "But how?"

"We go in the direction he was traveling," I said. "We spread out but not so far we can't hear each other. We yell his name, look for footprints, beat the bushes. He'll turn up."

"I can carry a little extra food for when we find him," the Loon said. "I see you found his pants."

"I've got an aversion to seeing other dude's junk," I said. "Must have been something in my upbringing."

"I'll keep that in mind," he said. "In case Chickadee wants to go skinny dipping."

"Let's hit the trail," I said. "Once we get away from the campsites, we'll start yelling for him."

"Everyone ready?" Brody asked.

We all nodded in the affirmative.

"Let's roll," said the Loon.

# Two

The New River flows north in Ashe County, North Carolina, into Virginia. I've heard it's the only major river in the United States to flow north. I don't know if that's true or not, but we followed it north looking for Bobbie. We gradually fanned out and started calling his name. I was closest to the river, thinking that's where he would be. Brody was roughly one hundred yards to my left. The others were similarly staggered to the left of her. The Loon was farthest away from the river. I couldn't hear him yell, but I could hear his wife and everyone else. I kept looking for a bare footprint in the mud beside the river. I kept an eye on Brody, so we didn't wander too far apart.

We assumed that all the noise we were making would deter bears and that Bobbie would hear us sooner or later. None of us thought that it would take long to find him, but as the day wore on, our thinking began to change. Sometime after noon, I called everyone together so we could take a break. We took stock of our supplies. We'd only brought enough water and snacks to last the day. If we didn't find him in the next few hours, we'd be forced to turn back. We didn't want to get stuck out there in the dark. We had more supplies back at camp to get us through the night.

"You think maybe we ought to call the authorities?" asked Loon.

"I do," said Chickadee. "Figured we'd have got him by now."

"Any chance he's hiding from us due to all the racket?" Brody asked. "Maybe he thinks we want to arrest him."

"I'll defer to Jessie Lynn," I said. "She knows him."

"He went berserk," said Jessie. "The drugs made him crazy. He's not like that. He's a curious sort, kind of sensitive. Always talking about nature and stuff. He's got to be afraid right now, which is all the more reason we need to find him."

"He's never done anything like this before?" I asked.

"Never," she said. "He doesn't even do drugs, other than a puff of weed if someone offers it."

"He was at a dead run when we saw him," I said. "If he kept that up for long he could still be miles north of us. How're everyone's legs holding up?"

I secretly wished that someone would say they'd had enough. My knees were holding out, but I was about to push them more than I wanted to. I didn't want to be the one to beg for mercy, though. I didn't get my wish. The Loon and the Chickadee reported that they were fine and willing to go on. Jessie was eager to continue. Brody gave me a look of concern, reading my mind in regards to my knees. I used the last of the bottle of water I was drinking to wash down two Ibuprofen.

"Let's find him," I said. "Keep up the chatter."

We spread out again and continued our trek north. I hoped that Bobbie hadn't strayed so far from the river that he couldn't hear us. He would definitely want a drink. His thirst would drive him to the river. If we had to turn around and go back, we could look farther west on the return trip. We hiked for two more hours, yelling his name at intervals. Where was he?

Finally, I decided that we'd strayed far enough from camp. We'd be pushed to make it back by dark, even if we hurried. I made my way to Brody's side, and together we met up with the other three. After a short rest, we redeployed farther west and started our march back. After a few hours, my knees started to give me warning signs. They weren't screaming, but I could feel some tenderness creeping in. I didn't like it, but it was to be expected. I'd done too much. I got close enough to Brody to talk without yelling.

"I'm going to slow down," I told her. "I'll be stopping and resting too. Stay with the others in case Bobbie turns up."

"I hate to leave you behind," she said. "You won't make it back before dark."

"I'll be fine," I said. "Mountain man and all that shit."

"We're going to have to call in the police," she said.

"They'll call me and ask me to bring Red out here," I said. "I don't think I'll be able to keep up with him."

We had boarded our hound dog at the vet in Banner Elk. The girls there loved him and spoiled him rotten. He was normally part of our team, but this camping trip wasn't a good fit. He would have to be kept on a leash and sleep in the tent with us. Brody didn't allow him in our bed, let alone in our sleeping bag.

"Go ahead without me," I said. "Keep the others out from the river. Keep calling for Bobbie."

"See you back at camp," she said.

I rested and cursed my knees for a few minutes. Getting old was a bitch. I'd been trying to come to terms with it lately, with little success. I had no time for weakness. I had shit to do. I started walking again at a slower pace, taking care not to stress my aching joints. I also started to hear better without the noise of the rest of my team. I started picking up on the scents of the woods too. I let it come to me, feeling the vibrations of the woods and the river. Now that I was alone, I could get a better feel for what was happening around me. I hadn't thought that I'd need to go all Zen to find a naked tripper, but I went with it anyway. If I was going to move slowly, I could at least take advantage of the skills that I possessed.

After two hours, I heard something that was not natural to the forest. I stopped and listened more intently. I heard it again. It was a muffled sobbing sound off to my right, barely audible. I zeroed in on it and tracked it down. Tucked up under a low hanging pine was a naked man, snuffling into his hands.

"It's okay, Bobbie," I said. "I'm here to help. Are you hurt?"

"The Moon-eyed People, man," he said. "They were everywhere."

"Moon-eyed People?"

"All over these woods," he said. "Up and down the hill."

"Are they here now?"

"They only come out at night," he said. "They were carrying rocks up the hill from the river."

"Are you still tripping?"

"I'm not tripping, man," he said. "You said you were here to help me."

"I've got your pants," I said, tossing them to him. "We need to get you back to Jessie Lynn. She's worried sick about you."

He came out of hiding, wearing the jeans. I gave him water and a granola bar. He kept telling me about the Moon-eyed People, insisting that what he saw was not drug-induced.

"They carried the rocks up there," he said, pointing. "Come on; I'll show you."

I followed him up the hill where we found rocks stacked in a line about ten feet long and two feet high. They were smooth like river rocks and obviously placed by hand. It was a curious sight, given Bobbie's story, but I was sure there was some reasonable explanation.

"See?" he said. "I'm telling you the truth."

"Let's get back to the campsite," I told him. "Get you warm by the fire and put some dinner in you. Jessie will be relieved that you're okay."

"You believe me, don't you?" he asked.

"I believe that you think you saw something."

"I was coming down when I saw them," he said. "I don't know what the deal was with those mushrooms, but I wasn't tripping all night long."

"Somebody dropped you some acid," I told him. "Let that be a lesson to you."

"I only did it because it was supposed to be an organic high," he said. "People told me it was a nice experience."

"It should have been," I said. "But you got punked."

"Fuck," he said.

"You scared the hell out of your girlfriend and put several other people out," I said. "You'll be apologizing when we get back, understand?"

"I am sorry," he said. "I wasn't expecting anything like what happened."

"Follow me," I said. "I'm moving a little slow, but we'll get there."

By the time we made camp, I'd had enough of my knees whining, and enough of the Moon-eyed People. Jessie ran out to hug Bobbie and wrapped him in her sleeping bag. The Loon had some meat cooking over the fire and a bottle of brandy by his side. Brody kissed me and asked how I was doing.

"I wish we could go home now," I said. "But I'm not canoeing out of here in the dark. Booze and Advil will have to hold me until morning."

"Coming up," she said. "Go sit by the fire."

I pulled up a stump and sat next to the Loon.

"Where was he?" he asked.

"A natural hut under a pine," I told him. "We passed close by it this morning."

"He must have been asleep," he said.

"Maybe so," I said. "He keeps rambling on about little white people with big eyes."

"Moon-eyed People?"

"How did you know?" I asked.

"We did some research on local lore before we came down here," he explained. "Read about the Cherokee legends. The story of the Moon-eyes caught our attention."

"Bobbie claims to have seen them firsthand," I said. "Says he was no longer high when it happened."

"This trip just got a lot more interesting," he said. "Excuse me while I talk to the boy."

Brody brought me what was left of the whiskey. I sat staring at the fire, listening to Bobbie tell the Loon all about the Moon-eyed People. His hallucination involved intricate details that could only have been produced by LSD. The Loon, however, seemed fascinated. The Chickadee was listening intently as well. These people were very white, with hair that was so blond it was almost white too. They had big blue eyes that shone in the dim moonlight. They wore flowing robes that made them appear ghostlike. They were all busy gathering rocks and transporting them up the hill. Bobbie watched from his hiding spot, too afraid to move.

"Not that I believe any of this," I said. "But I saw a wall of rocks up the hill from where I found him."

The Loon tried to convince Bobbie to take him to see those rocks the next day. Bobbie and Jessie just wanted to go home. He turned and looked at me.

"I want to go home too," I said. "I can try to give you directions, but that's the best I can do."

"If the rock wall is there like you say it is," he said. "I might want to move our camp near there and see these little people myself."

"You'll need more than brandy to see them," I said. "Ask Bobbie if he has any more magic mushrooms."

"I threw them in the river with the rest of our stuff," Bobbie said. "There was bad juju in those things."

"Maybe the Moon-eyed People will find them," I said. "They'll be seeing naked humans hiding under every tree."

"I saw what I saw," he said. "I'm sorry to be of nuisance to you. I want to thank you for coming for me."

"Apologize to your girlfriend," I said. "If we weren't here, she would have had a rough time of it."

He got up with the sleeping bag still wrapped around him and went to Jessie Lynn. They hugged tightly for a minute.

"I'm so sorry, baby," he said. "I won't do anything like that again. Not even dope. I swear it."

"It will be okay," she said. "We'll get out of here tomorrow and go back home."

"You probably shouldn't go around telling everyone about the little people you saw in the woods," I said. "Wouldn't want folks to think you've gone crazy."

"Take your tent and go with your friend here," Bobbie said. "You'll see."

"You're welcome to come along," The Loon said.

"No thanks," I said. "This trip is over in the morning."

We didn't bother with cooking breakfast. We packed up our stuff and loaded the canoe at first light. We exchanged contact information with our new friends before shoving off and paddling back to the park office. We stopped at the Cracker Barrel in Boone to get some food before driving to Banner Elk to pick up our hound dog Red. He practically licked the stubble off my face when they let him out. I hugged him and rubbed behind his ears until he finally settled down. Brody took care of the bill while I took him out to the car. He was as ready to go home as we were.

I let him run around the yard once we got to the cabin. He marked his favorite spots to reestablish his territory before we went inside. It wasn't long before he was lying on the rug in front of the fireplace. I propped my tired legs up in the recliner instead of unloading our gear.

"I'll get it later," I told Brody. "Just leave it for now."

"How are your bones?" she asked.

"Not horrible," I said. "I didn't wreck them again, but I think I pushed them right up to their limit."

"You would have been fine if we didn't have to organize a search party for a fool," she said.

"He was damn lucky for that," I said. "Could have gone bad for them otherwise."

"You're either in the right place at the right time, or the wrong place at the wrong time," she said. "I'm not sure which."

"At least there were no dead bodies involved this time," I said.

"You're going to need to rest those old knees again," she said. "We'll find some flat ground to explore when you're feeling better."

"Flat ground is a rare thing in the High Country."

"We can walk around the park," she said. "Get you some good walking shoes. Build you back up before we hit the mountains again."

"We live on a mountain."

"Don't be stubborn," she said. "You need to take this seriously, or you won't be able to do shit."

She was right. There wasn't much point to living here if I couldn't enjoy all the things that I loved about the area. I'd been trying to turn myself into a mountain man, and had done a good job of it, but if I wanted that to continue, I needed to manage the arthritis in my knees. It sucked getting old. If my knees didn't improve, I might as well move back to Florida. Walking in the sand was a good workout, and there were no hills.

"While I'm sitting here doing nothing," I said. "Why don't you look up those Moon People that Bobbie was talking about?"

"Moon-eyed People," she said. "He was very specific about that."

"Let's see what the internet has to say about them."

Red came and begged to be rubbed while Brody asked Google about the Moon-eyed People. I stroked his smooth fur from my position in the recliner. He wanted me to get down on the floor with him like I normally would, but my knees nixed that idea.

"It's a real thing," Brody said. "At least the legend is."

"The Cherokee thing?"

"Yes, they said that little white people inhabited these lands before the Indians arrived," she said. "Eventually the Cherokee ran them off or killed them."

"Where's the Moon-eyed part come in?"

"They only came out at night," she said. "Couldn't see in the daytime. These descriptions are exactly like Bobbie's."

"I'm guessing Bobbie has read the same story," I said. "Or heard the legend passed down over the generations."

"Come look at this," she said. "This is a sandstone sculpture on display at the Cherokee History Museum."

The picture showed two little people, about three feet tall, with huge eyes. They were conjoined like Siamese twins. It was found in the 1840s near Murphy, North Carolina. It meshed nicely with the legend we were discussing, but hardly convinced me. It did arouse my curiosity.

"What do you think?" I asked.

"Myth based on some reality," she said. "Embellished over hundreds of years."

"What's the real part?" I asked. "Little people, big-eyed people, white-skinned people?"

"Albinos maybe," she said.

"Albinos that only come out at night," I said. "Aliens landed at Roswell."

"Aren't you the least bit curious?"

"Sure," I said. "But let's stay rational about this. There is probably a reasonable explanation for the legend."

"I'll go consult the local Cherokee medicine man," she said.

"Ask him why his people killed all the little people."

# THREE

Very few people had my phone number. Our circle of friends was a total of two people, both police officers. Various departments in the area could call me if they needed a tracker or a hound dog. My buddy Rominger was with the North Carolina Highway Patrol. Angelina Will worked for the Avery County Sheriff's Office. She and I had flirted with disaster when we first met, but I couldn't bring myself to cheat on the woman I loved. Since then, we'd become friends. We worked together on a suspicious death, cementing our relationship. Brody was not threatened by her; in fact, the two of them got along nicely.

When my phone rang, and the display showed an unfamiliar number, I almost didn't answer it.

"Hello?"

"Breeze, this is Linwood," said the voice on the other end.

"Linwood?"

"The Loon," he said. "From New River."

"Oh, hey," I said. "Sorry about that. What's up?"

"I just thought you'd like to know that we spent two nights camped near that rock pile," he said. "Not a single little white person was spotted."

"I think you were missing the necessary pharmaceuticals for that," I said. "Interesting that you would try."

"It's a hobby of sorts for us," he said. "There are tons of old myths floating about Maine, you know."

"Give me the highlights," I said.

"Most pertinent would be our own version of little people, also an Indian legend," he said.

"Think there is any relation?"

"Our little people were more like fairies, leprechauns, or hobbits," he said. "They are supposed to be all around us, but some just can't see them."

"That part parallels our Moon-eyes," I said. "Can't have a good myth without a little mystery."

"We have the Monster of Pocomoonshine Lake, the Cherryfield Goatman, and the Ghost on Catherine's Hill," he said. Throw in some Sasquatch and a little Paul Bunyon and that about covers it."

"We had the Hook Man where I grew up," I said. "He was alleged to harass teenagers necking in Blackbird Forest."

"Did you believe it when you were young?"

"I looked for girls brave enough to make out with me in that forest," I said. "Just to prove he didn't exist."

"Seems like that would narrow the field," he said.

"You'd be surprised."

"Anyway, we are planning a trip down to the Cherokee History Museum to view the little people sculpture. Any chance you'd like to come with us?"

"Hang on," I said. "Hey, Brody, you want to go see that Moony People statue?"

"Moon-eyed People," she said. "Sure. Who's that?"

"The Loon and the Chickadee want us to go with them," I said.

"Okay."

"We're in," I told the Loon.

"Great," he said. "We'll pick you up tomorrow morning."

I gave him our address and some rough directions to the cabin. We were off the beaten path, but not impossible to find. He said they'd arrive mid-morning. I hung up and thought about having guests to our place. It was a rare thing for us. I wondered if they'd want to spend the night after our trip to the museum. No one had ever stayed overnight with us. We did have an extra bedroom. They might appreciate a hot shower after a week in the woods. I told Brody to consider that possibility.

"Houseguests," she said. "What a novel idea."

"I know you've wanted to make new friends," I said. "But they live in Maine. It will just be temporary."

"You never know when we might need a friend in Maine," she said.

"I've been up there several times," I said. "But only in August. I don't see a reason to go back."

"We should do some traveling," she said. "We've got free time."

"There are people out there in the real world," I told her. "Lots of people."

"I understand what you're saying," she said. "But I'm not as anti-social as you are. We really need to get out more. Expand our horizons."

"Bah, humbug," I said. "Get off of my lawn."

"Be nice tomorrow," she said. "It's a chance for us to be around other people."

"I like the Loon," I said. "At least I did out in the woods. Not too sure about his fascination with myths, though."

"Not everything is black and white," she said. "Let yourself indulge in a little mystery."

"Mystery to me is what lacy panties you have on, and how can I get them off?" I said.

"Play along with our fantasy tomorrow," she said. "Then, maybe I'll make your fantasy come true."

"It's always good to have the proper incentive," I said. "Challenge accepted."

Loon and Chickadee pulled up around ten the next morning. They drove a frigging Subaru like everyone else in the High Country. It was packed to the gills with camping gear. I had unloaded our Ford Escape before they arrived, so I suggested we take our car. My offer was quickly accepted. It was a three and a half hour drive to Murphy, North Carolina so we took off right away. Brody kept up polite conversation with them while I drove in silence. I was calculating how long our day was going to be. Seven hours of driving the roundtrip, plus an hour or two in the museum, meant that we'd get back home sometime around seven that night. Red could make it that long, but not much longer.

The museum itself wasn't what I expected. It was on the small side, but packed wall to wall with artifacts and exhibits. The people working there were friendly and eager to talk about anything you wanted to know. There were many Indian artifacts, and an entire lesson to be learned about the Trail of Tears. The Moon-eyed People sculpture was the highlight of the entire experience. I stood in front of the display case and became engrossed in an aura that I couldn't explain. Seeing that carving made it all seem real to me. I had to admit to the others in my group that I'd gained a new interest in this particular legend.

"Is there a camping trip to a certain rock pile in your future?" asked the Loon.

"I'm not going that far," I said. "But I'll give the myth some credence. This statue is something real, not just an old wives tale."

"I'm glad you see it that way," he said. "Nothing wrong with believing in fairy tales now and then. Adds a little magic to life."

We spent almost two hours in the museum before finally heading back home. The ladies carried the conversation on the return trip. Our guests would be happy to take advantage of our offer to spend the night, take hot showers, and have a home-cooked meal. After letting Red out, I started a fire in the fireplace. It wasn't for the heat, but the ambiance. We weren't in the woods, but we could watch the flames dance while we shot the shit.

"So you say that chasing these myths is a hobby for you?" I asked the Loon.

"It adds another dimension to exploring," he said. "I can't remember how we ever got started chasing legends, but we've been doing it for a long time."

"Have you ever witnessed anything, or found any information that would verify any of them?"

"Not in the slightest," he said. "It's like trying to grab a handful of fog on the coast of Maine."

"But you keep doing it," I said. "Just for fun."

"The truth is out there," he said. "Or maybe not."

"I was interested in UFOs when I was a kid," I told him. "Guess I outgrew it."

"Life beats the curiosity right out of us," he said. "We stop believing."

"I think we learn that magic isn't real and that fairy tales don't come true."

"Scratch any cynic, and you'll find a disappointed idealist," he said.

"We were all liberal, idealistic, and dumb in our youth," I said. "We age into conservatism and realism."

"Either that or we trade our dreams for whatever wisdom age brings."

"This is becoming a most philosophical discussion," I said. "Socrates or Plato?"

"George Carlin," he said. "Much more than a funny man."

"So how would one go about reigniting the curiosity of our youth?"

"Excellent question," he said. "It indicates that you are not a lost cause."

"I think there have been too many times when my only cause was staying alive," I said. "Not much time to chase dreams."

"Nonsense," Brody interrupted. "You once had a dream to share beautiful islands with a woman who loved you. Check that one off. Then you wanted a cabin in the woods. Check that off too. If you dream a new dream, we can make it happen."

"Perfectly valid points," I said. "But we're talking about myths, legends, and UFOs."

"The Beech Mountain Hermit was a legend," she said. "Until you proved he was real."

"You had a hermit here?" asked the Loon. "In the mountains?"

"Sure did," I said. "Still, do actually, but I don't know where he is now."

"How did you prove his existence?"

"I went out in the woods and found him," I said. "He was a witness in a murder case. We needed him to testify. In the end, he returned to the wilderness, and I left him alone."

"You must be one hell of a tracker," he said.

"I had some help from Brody and Red."

"We had a most famous hermit case not far from where we live," he began. "Christopher Knight lived without human contact for twenty-seven years. He was called the North Pond Hermit."

"I've heard about him," I said. "Similar case. Our guy robbed unoccupied cabins for necessities, but never took much of value. No one ever spotted him."

"Same with ours," he said. "Half his victims sympathized with him. The other half wanted him caught and jailed."

"What happened to him?"

"He was finally caught by a game warden. Trail cams did him in," he said. "He served seven months in jail and was ordered to attend some sort of therapy. His brother gave him a job back in the real world. There was a bestselling book written about the whole affair."

"Interesting, but a bit sad, don't you think?"

"It has a Ralph Waldo Emerson feel to it," he said. "Who also didn't stay in the woods forever."

"But now he's working nine to five," I said. "Probably has a car loan and credit cards."

"Don't we all?"

"We don't," I said. "Our only bills are utilities and these damn phones."

"That makes you unique in American Society," he said.

"I've had some unique experiences," I said. "Some beautiful and fascinating. Some ugly and dangerous."

"You seem to be happy in the place you are now."

"That's because of Brody," I told him. "She gave me a purpose in life."

"As Betty did for me."

"Betty?"

"Chickadee," he said. "When we're not on the trails, we're Linwood and Betty."

"I'll stick with Breeze and Brody," I said. "Has a nice ring to it."

"Indeed it does," he said. "Now, can you see the possibility of letting a little mystery into your life? If not Moon-eyed People, then maybe something else."

"I think I follow you," I said. "Maybe I can let myself be a little more open to things I can't explain."

"Atta boy," he said. "We'll turn you into an explorer yet."

"Breeze is so set in his ways you'd think he was eighty-years-old," Brody said.

"I feel like I have eighty-year-old knees lately," I said. "I won't be hunting Sasquatch until that changes."

"Walking sticks are helpful on hills," the Loon said. "Drink more water and less booze."

"My friends in this order," I said. "Are Brody, Red, and booze."

"You can add Betty and me to your list," he said. "You're always welcome to visit."

"I appreciate that," I said. "I'll let you know if I ever catch an alien in these mountains."

"You never know."

The fire died down, and the conversation dimmed with it. After a quick trip out back with Red, it was time to turn in. I fell asleep quickly and dreamt of weird creatures in the woods. The trolls, goblins, and goat men were not evil beings seeking my death. They were going about the business of existing, just like everyone else. We fixed a big country breakfast for our friends in the morning, and they left soon after eating. They were bound for West Virginia to learn more about the Mothman.

"So, are you to become a supernatural sleuth now?" Brody asked.

"I thought all of you were encouraging me to be more open-minded about such things."

"You can be too serious about life at times," she said. "Wouldn't hurt for you to have a little fun."

"You think that hunting for things that don't exist will be fun?"

"The museum was pretty cool," she said. "You said the sculpture interested you."

"I guess it did," I said. "Made the myth seem tangible to me."

"Do you want to learn more about the Moon-eyed People?" she asked.

"The Cherokee were in Appalachia as early as 1700," I said. "Talk about a cold case. I assume that whatever can be learned has already been discovered."

"Then we'll pick a new myth to examine," she said. "Any ideas?"

"The Brown Mountain Lights," I said. "We can drive to the Brown Mountain Overlook, pack some snacks and drinks, and wait for the lights to appear."

"How do you know when they can be seen?"

"You don't," I said. "That's the thing. It's like the Green Flash. Watch a thousand sunsets to catch a glimpse of it once."

"Have you seen the Green Flash?"

"Several times," I said. "But I was on the water watching the sunset every day for many years. Your casual beachgoer or vacationer will likely never see it."

"Some don't believe it's real," she said.

"It's clearly a real phenomenon," I told her. "I've seen it with my own eyes."

"So you believed in a myth."

"It's not a myth."

"You know what I mean," she said. "Something otherworldly that you witnessed. You believed."

"So I should believe in little white people?"

"Do you believe in the Brown Mountain Lights?"

"I do, though I've not seen them yet," I said. "I guess I see what you're getting at."

"How far is this Overlook?"

"There are a couple of different spots where they can be seen," I said. "Wisemans View and the Lost Cove Overlook are two others. Maybe an hour from here."

"Okay," she said. "Let's do it. What are our odds of seeing the lights?"

"Slim," I said.

"What causes them?"

"That hasn't been determined actually," I said. "Even though researchers and scientists have tried."

"So how do you know they are real?"

"They've been seen thousands of times," I said. "Even by the Cherokee."

"You've got my interest," she said. "We'll do it."

We made our first trip to the Brown Mountain Overlook a few days later. The car was loaded with beer, cheese and crackers, and one hound dog. We arrived just after dark and sat watching the mountain until after midnight. No mysterious lights showed themselves. We tried again a week later with the same results. We tried the other viewing spots several times over the course of two weeks, but we still didn't see the lights. We got discouraged and gave up the pursuit for a while. Later we learned that the best time to see them was in the fall. Brody wrote on the calendar so we would remember to try again in October, preferably after a rain.

In the meantime, something was afoot in Banner Elk that prompted the Chief of Police to give me a call. Some jackasses had been vandalizing graveyards. Three different cemeteries had been hit in two weeks. The police department couldn't afford to station an officer at each one all night long. It would detract from their real job of protecting the citizens of the town.

"I know it's kind of bullshit work," the Chief said. "But do you think you could stake out these sites for a little while? Maybe we'll get lucky and catch the bastards quickly."

"Sure, Chief," I said. "We've resorted to looking for the Brown Mountain Lights for something to do lately."

"I tried to see them a couple of times," he said. "Didn't see anything either."

"Give me the particulars," I said. "We'll get right on this."

The vandals had hit the Banner Elk Cemetery, the Potts Cemetery, and the Lowe Family Cemetery. Multiple headstones had been destroyed or knocked over. It was a senseless crime that could only hurt the families of the deceased. Everyone assumed it was the work of college students. No one thought that locals would commit such a heinous act of disrespect.

Before we set up surveillance the first night, I had Brody do a little research into other graveyards in the area. I took a chance in thinking that the assholes would hit some other place rather than return to the scenes of the original crimes. I didn't tell the Chief, but we set up the first night at Fox Cemetery. It was the closest target to the other three. Nothing happened. On the second night, we split up and watched the Michael and the Yates Cemeteries. Nothing happened. It was incredibly boring duty, but we were getting paid and doing a favor for the Chief.

On the third night, we split up once again. I was stationed back at Fox, while Brody hid in the Michael Cemetery. I had visitors just before midnight. I called the Chief to send officers and continued to watch the intruders. Three male suspects of college age began kicking at headstones and laughing. It was a disgusting display of ignorance. Some of the stones withstood the onslaught. Others broke or fell over. I waited for a cop to arrive, anxious to bust these jerks. As soon as I saw headlights approaching, I sprung to action, shining a light on the vandals and yelling for them to stop. They all took off in the same direction. I gave chase, yelling for the cop to follow me. As soon as the officer caught up, I fell back. I hadn't hurt my knees, and I didn't want to. Besides, I was being paid for surveillance, not for a foot chase.

I did not, however, let down my guard. Instead, I took a different route, walking rather than running. Sure enough, one of the suspects had left his buddies and circled back to make his escape. I was there to knock the shit out of him and encourage him to remain still until the officer returned. The cop came back with one kid in cuffs. I instructed my captive to follow the nice officer to his patrol car. We'd physically captured two out of three, which ain't bad. The perps would give up their friend in no time. I made sure both were in the backseat of the cop car before relaxing. My work here was done. I called Brody to come pick me up.

# FOUR

Over the next month, no jobs came our way. We hadn't picked another legend to investigate. I took regular trips to the park in Valle Crucis, which had a walking path entirely on flat ground. Red accompanied me, and we took leisurely strolls along the Watauga River to work my arthritic knees without taxing them too hard. I was taking turmeric every day, drinking less booze, and generally feeling healthier. Winter was well behind us now. Spring flowers and rhododendrons were in full bloom. The trout were biting in the lakes and rivers. It was time to enjoy the High Country in all its splendor.

I was farting around in the garage one day and came across our old SAT phone. I took it inside and plugged it in to charge. It was supposed to be our lifeline to our old friend Captain Fred down in Florida. We'd forgotten about it once we bought cell phones. There were only a handful of people who had the number, so unless Fred had tried to contact us, I didn't expect anything to be on it. It had multiple special features, including its untraceable quality. Fred had an affinity for security, especially with his communications. He wouldn't email anything important and often wanted to talk in person in some safe place if he had important business to take care of. I'd once flown to St. Petersburg, Florida and boarded a charter boat just to spend thirty minutes talking to him. Our conversation didn't begin until we were miles offshore, and the captain was preoccupied.

I decided to get his number off the SAT phone and give him a call to let him know we now had phones of our own. He didn't answer, and there was no messaging capability. I could only hope that he'd see our North Carolina area code and realize it was us that had called him. A few days went by with no return call, and I forgot all about it. I did leave the phone on and charging just in case. I think subconsciously I wanted him to call and ask for my help with something. The mountain life was quite pleasant in the spring, but I was getting antsy for some kind of action. I felt like a thoroughbred that had been relegated to giving pony rides to kids at the county fair. Staking out cemeteries didn't really do it for me. Sitting around, hoping to see the Brown Mountain Lights was boring as well.

Another week passed before the damn thing rang. I was sitting quietly reading a book, so the noise startled me. It took a few seconds to figure out where it was coming from. I didn't recognize the number but answered it anyway.

"Breeze," I said.

"It's Daniel," he said. "Daniel Ames."

"I hope you're well, Marine," I said. "I didn't realize you had this number."

"I had to do some work to get it," he said. "Captain Fred gave it to me."

"Are you in trouble?"

"Not me," he said. "It's Holly."

Daniel and Holly were names from my past. Holly had been my sometimes lover and partner for several years. We'd been through one adventure after another together. We'd dove for gold on behalf of an old lady who ended up dying before we could make her rich. I'd suffered a broken rib thanks to an angry hammerhead shark during that one. We'd helped another old treasure hunter recover his stolen gold down in the Keys. Holly had followed him down to Guatemala and Belize to continue the treasure hunt. Daniel had sailed off with her at one point, only to return alone within the year. I'd given him a sailboat that I'd bought from a couple who couldn't afford to keep it or fix it up.

I had treated Daniel like the son I never had, teaching him the ways of the sea. He spent some time finding himself living on a boat in Florida, but it wasn't his future to keep doing that. He took a position with a veteran's group called Enduring Warrior in Virginia. I hadn't spoken to him much since then.

I had a special place in my heart for Holly. We'd tried to find a way to love each other as we each deserved, but our age difference was the deal breaker. She was twenty years younger, pretty, and adventurous. I couldn't hold her back forever. She sailed off alone on her sailboat to points unknown, but far away. Now Daniel was calling me on her behalf. Something serious was going on.

"Is she okay?" I asked.

"She's busted up pretty bad," he said. "She needs help. I've got a career now, and I can't leave."

"Where is she?"

"In a hospital in Tortola," he said.

"The BVI?"

"Yes," he said. "Her boat is anchored out with no one to watch out for it. She got run over in her dinghy by a big cabin cruiser. She said the boat wasn't properly prepared for bad weather. The hatches might even be open. She doesn't have much money either. She's in a bad way, Breeze."

"What are her injuries?"

"Broken ribs which punctured a lung," he began. "They got a tube in her chest, and she's on oxygen. Her arm is botched up too. Her dinghy is destroyed."

"Where is she on Tortola?"

"It's called Peebles Hospital, in Road Town," he said. "Can you help her?"

"I don't see why not," I said. "Does she know you are calling me?"

"She does," he said. "She didn't know where else to turn."

"I appreciate you going out of your way to track me down," I said. "You doing okay?"

"I'm fine, man," he said. "We'll catch up later."

"Okay, good," I said. "Let me give you my cell phone number for future reference."

"Where are you?" he asked.

"Blue Ridge Mountains," I said. "Come visit when you get a chance."

"You sold *Leap of Faith*?" he asked.

"Long story," I said. "We've got a log cabin now."

"Son of a bitch."

"Give me Holly's number," I said.

I saved both Holly's and Daniel's numbers in my phone and went to tell Brody what was going on. I wasn't sure how she'd react.

"You should go right away," she said. "I'll make the flight arrangements for you. Start packing."

"You're not coming with me?"

"We've got Red to take care of," she said. "You need to be fast on your feet. I'll stay and hold down the fort. You go."

"Are you sure about this?"

"Get packing," she said. "Warm weather clothes and any gear you think you need, but keep it as light as you can."

I did as I was told. Brody yelled to me from the computer.

"Change over in Puerto Rico or St. Thomas?" she asked.

Many years ago, I had flown into Puerto Rico on my way to Tortola with my first wife, Laura. The airport there was the worst I'd ever experienced. I preferred not to go through there again.

"St. Thomas," I said. "As long as it doesn't delay me too long."

"There's a non-stop from Charlotte on American," she said. "We can make it if we hurry."

"Book it," I said.

I almost threw my gun in the bag but decided it wasn't worth the hassle that it would cause. I had shorts and lightweight shirts but couldn't find my flip flops. I grabbed a handful of clean boxers and tossed them in the bag. It was hard to think clearly. Holly was in trouble, and I was too rushed. *Calm down, Breeze.*

I would just have to buy whatever I forgot when I got there, or do without. Brody had the car running when I was ready. I jumped in the passenger seat, and we took off for Charlotte. It was a little over two hours away. We had three hours before departure. Brody drove well above the speed limit until we were certain that we'd make it. I got a quick kiss before she shoved me out of the car.

"Call me when you can," she said.

"Love you," I said.

"Love you, too," she said. "Go take care of business."

I got my boarding pass and hustled to the gate. The line at security was thankfully a short one. I slid through with no problems; handing my pass to the attendant and boarding the plane without a wait. I could finally relax. I felt naked with no weapons and very little belongings with me. I had my phone and wallet, which was stuffed with cash. I had my wits. I also had the advantage of having been to Tortola previously. I knew that I'd wait for Customs for too long and that there would probably be dogs or chickens wandering about the airport, maybe both. There would be no car waiting for me because I wasn't checking into a resort, but there would be a taxi eager to take my American money.

I wasn't familiar with the hospital. Should I go there first or tend to Holly's boat? I realized that I didn't know where her boat was anchored. I'd visit her first. *Another Adventure* would have to wait until I checked on Holly and got a better grasp of the situation. I lay back in my seat as much as it would allow and told myself to chill out. The flight lasted almost four hours, and I still had another short hop to Beef Island. Small planes flew back and forth from St. Thomas and Puerto Rico several times per day.

It was six in the evening before I landed. Luckily, the Customs employee was waiting for this last flight to land before he could go home. He checked us in quickly with zero scrutiny. The airport was otherwise empty. I walked outside and found one lone cabbie sleeping at the wheel. I tapped on the car, startling him.

"Peebles Hospital?" I asked.

"Sure, man," he said. "It's down by the harbor. Twenty bucks."

I was in no position to haggle about the fare. He was my only shot at a ride. I gave him a crisp twenty and got in the passenger side, which was on the left of the car, where the steering wheel should have been. We drove on the wrong side of the road at too great a speed into Road Town. That car ride was much more frightening than either of the plane rides.

"You need me to wait?" he asked.

"I might be a while," I said. "But I will call you if you're going to be on duty later."

"Where do you want to go next?"

"I don't know yet," I said.

He wrote down his number and said he'd be available until nine.

"Thanks, pal," I said.

I went inside to the help desk and asked for Holly's room number. By pure chance, I had arrived during the evening visiting hours. I found her sitting up in bed, staring at some unidentifiable food on a tray table. I tapped on the door.

"Holly."

She turned to look at me.

"Wait. What?" she said. "There is no freaking way that Breeze is standing there looking at me. I must be over-medicated."

"You're good," I said. "It's me."

"I don't even know what to say," she said. "Daniel told me he would try to get in touch with you, but I never expected you to show up."

"I heard an old friend needed my help," I said. "Now, tell me that you're going to be okay."

"Other than the heart attack you just gave me, I'm supposed to recover."

"Fill me in and tell me what you need me to do first," I said. "I'm at your service."

"When you come back bring me a cheese-burger," she said. "I'm so sick of beans and rice."

"What happened, Holly?"

"I got in the dink after dark with no lights," she said. "I had a headlamp on, but that was it. I got ran the fuck over, Breeze."

"Ouch," I said. "How bad is the damage?"

"My little dinghy is destroyed," she said. "I'm busted up. *Another Adventure* is riding a short rode with the main hatch and all the port lights open. Probably being robbed as we speak."

"Where is she?"

"Nanny Cay," she said. "Out from the yacht club."

"Is there a water taxi?"

"This is the BVI," she said. "Not Annapolis."

"I'll find another dinghy then," I said. "I'll secure your vessel as soon as I can get out there to it."

"That would be great," she said. "All I can do is sit here and worry."

She had a tube in her chest and oxygen to her nose. Her hair was gnarly, and she looked like hell, but I still saw her as the cute hippie chick that I'd always known, except now I felt much more like a father figure than a lover. Time had moved on for both of us.

"How much chain do you have out now?" I asked.

"Like fifty feet," she said. "The rest is rope. You'll need to put some chafe guard on it once you let more out."

"Keys?"

"In the ignition," she said. "I was just coming in for dinner."

"Short rode, keys left in the ignition, dinghy in the dark with no lights," I said. "You've gotten sloppy my friend."

"You taught me better," she said. "Guess I got cocky."

"We'll talk more about that once you get on your feet," I said. "I'll go tend to your boat now."

"Hug first?" she said. "Gently, of course."

I went to her and gave her the softest of hugs. She held me a few seconds longer than necessary.

"I can't believe you came for me," she said. "Thank you so much."

"You're going to be all right," I said. "Lay back and take it easy. I'll be back as soon as I can."

I hated to see her in such a frail condition. Her body was broken, but her spirit still shone through. She'd always been a risk taker, not that I hadn't taken risks myself. Mine were usually a result of careful calculation of the situation. Her's were more spur of the moment jump off bridges decisions. This time it had bitten her in the ass. She would survive, though, and be smarter for the experience.

I went out to the curb and found my taxi driver still parked in the same place. I guess he'd gotten no other fares while I visited Holly. He seemed glad to see me, knowing that his decision to wait had paid off.

"I need to buy a dinghy with a motor," I said. "Take me to that place."

"Moorings and Sun Sail likely have some old ones laying around," he said. "The motor is a different story."

"Something tells me that you know a guy," I said. "A guy that might have a motor for sale."

"The charter companies are closed for the night anyway," he said. "But I do know a guy."

"Let's go see him," I said.

Small outboards are gold in the islands. They are constantly being stolen from naïve sailors and charter customers. They're also in high demand. An unscrupulous character could make a decent living dealing in stolen outboards and dinghies. I was about to meet just such a character. He would ask too much, and I would protest, but the truth was that as a beggar I couldn't be choosy. If I was lucky, I could dicker him down a few hundred bucks.

# FIVE

My cabbie was named Frederick. He had curly wet hair and spoke with a distinct English accent. He charged me another twenty dollars to see a man about a dinghy. We pulled up in front of a dilapidated house in the worst section of Road Town. The front yard was stacked with old engine parts, cowlings, props, and assorted boat junk. My escort knocked and yelled at the same time.

"Hey, Charlie," he said. "I brought you a customer."

A very dark-skinned man opened the door and looked me over. He had pure white hair that clashed with his black skin, but what stood out were his massive hands and forearms. He looked like he'd lifted many motors in his day.

"This is a cash-only business, mister," he said.

"Not a problem," I said.

"What are you looking for?"

"Decent dinghy and a good outboard to go with it," I said. "Horsepower not important. I just need a good running motor."

"Follow me."

We walked through Charlie's house towards the back. The place was surprisingly neat, and no boat parts were seen. The back yard was a different story. It was surrounded by a high fence to shield his inventory from prying eyes. He had a dozen or so inflatables along with more than twenty small outboards.

"Good solid boats are here," he said. "I want a thousand a piece for any of these three."

"What's your best running motor?" I asked.

"This 9.9 Mercury runs like a raped ape," he said. "Old school two-stroke."

"I had one of those for a long time," I said. "What about these four-strokes?"

"This Yamaha is in the best shape," he said. "Runs good. Nice and quiet."

"How much?"

"Fifteen hundred," he said.

I took a closer look at the better dinghies. All three were Hypalon Caribes, the same as the big charter companies used. They were obviously stolen from rental customers who didn't know well enough to lock them up at night. They were good little boats and well-worth a grand. I pointed at the best looking one.

"I'll take this dink and the Yamaha," I said. "Will you take two thousand for the package?"

"That's five hundred out of my pocket," he said. "Dinghy man got to eat too, you know."

"Throw in one of these gas tanks, and I'll give you twenty-three hundred."

"This I can do," he said. "American cash, right?"

I pulled out my wallet and counted out 23 hundred dollar bills. I held it out for him to inspect. He was satisfied enough to take the money. He handed one of the bills to Frederick for his finder's fee. They had a good racket going.

"How can I get this rig down to the harbor?" I asked.

"I'll call for a truck," my cabbie said. "Cost you another, fifty."

"Do it."

Charlie dragged the chosen dinghy to a gate in the back fence. I picked up the Yamaha. It was heavier than I expected. I struggled to get a good grip before carrying it over and setting it down next to the dink. Frederick tossed an empty gas can in the boat.

"Truck is on its way," he said.

"Can I get gas down at the docks?"

"Too late tonight," Charlie said.

"I need to get out to a boat tonight," I told him.

"Plenty of little boats with gas tanks down there," he said. "You'll figure something out."

"Or wait until morning," Frederick added.

I wasn't going to wait all night for the gas dock to open. That was out of the question. We all heard the truck pull up, and we worked quickly to load my new boat and motor. Frederick didn't want anyone to see what was going on. I gave him a quick handshake and hopped in the passenger side of the truck. I waved to Frederick. My driver was a white man, much to my surprise. I guess a white man would be the only person on the island to own a pickup truck.

"The name's Breeze," I told him.

"I only care about the money," he said.

I handed him the fifty bucks.

"I can't put you in near the main charter docks," he said. "We'll slide this boat in the water in a dark place. You're on your own after that."

"You wouldn't happen to have any gasoline you could sell me, would you?"

"No, I do not," he said. "I'm just the freight hauler."

"Is there security around the charter fleet?"

"Moorings has a guard on the docks all night," he said. "Sun Sail has a guard too, but he likes to take a nap after he makes his rounds."

"What time is that?"

"Usually about ten," he said. "Stays in his shack for a couple hours."

"Will there be customers milling about?"

"Very few," he said. "They don't normally let them on the boat until morning. Makes them pay for a room the night before. A few more dollars to go around."

"Thanks," I said. "I think I can handle it."

"Where is your boat?"

"It's a friend's," I said. "Nanny Cay, near the yacht club."

"Can you find it in the dark?"

"I know the boat well," I said. "But not the water between here and there."

"It's a long ride in a dinghy," he said. "Especially in the dark. Hug the shore on your right as you exit the harbor. First big bay is Sea Cow Bay. That's not it. Second bay is for Nanny. The boats there are anchored off the resort. The Yacht Club is just a little further in. Nice protected anchorage."

"I appreciate it," I said.

"No problem," he said. "Good luck to you."

We pulled up to a seawall behind a warehouse. There were no lights. We worked together to carry the little boat down to the wall and slid it gently into the water. I tied it off and climbed down in it. My truck driving friend handed the motor down to me, and I secured it on the transom. He tossed me the gas can and untied me from the wall.

"Charter docks are that way," he said, pointing to the inner harbor.

Before I could get the oars situated, he was gone. I was on my own, just like he had said. I was back on the water, but not in a way that I would ever expect. I sat there in a little rubber boat, with no gas, in a foreign country. It was dark, and I wasn't sure where I was going. I started rowing in the direction he had pointed. I went slowly, trying to be quiet. As soon as I rounded a corner in the seawall, the sky lit up in front of me. A huge cruise ship was docked on the opposite side of the harbor. Hundreds of vessels were docked on my side. I remembered that the Moorings docks were first. Sun Sail had a few rows of docks further in on the same side. I rowed smoothly past the Moorings boats and stopped rowing as I approached the Sun Sail docks.

I looked for movement around the boats, but it was a ghost town. This part of the harbor was protected from the street. They had to keep the high-paying clientele separated from the realities of Road Town. I coasted along until I stopped. I floated, listening, and watching. There were indeed plenty of small boats like mine, but I needed to find one with a Yamaha so the gas connections would match. I eased up to a row of sailboats until I found what I needed. I quickly disconnected a gas tank from the motor and hoisted it into my boat. I replaced it with the one Charlie had provided, tucking a twenty under the handle to cover the cost of the gas I had just stolen. I took a quick look around again before making my escape.

As I rowed away from the charter docks, I couldn't help but think that it had been too easy. I was waiting for the blue lights to start flashing. The cops would arrive and arrest me, not only for stealing gas but for being in possession of a stolen boat and motor. That didn't happen. I felt that I was far enough away, and I was tired of rowing. I connected my new full gas tank, fiddled with the motor controls, and pulled the starter cord. It did not start on the first pull. I engaged the choke and tried again with no luck. I pulled that cord another dozen times before realizing that I hadn't put the kill switch on the motor. It was a stupid mistake, but not the first time I'd ever done it. After I got that right, the little motor fired right up. I killed the choke and gave it just enough gas to keep it running while it warmed up. I was in business, except for the lack of running lights. I was about to venture out into unfamiliar territory in the dark, with no lights. It was the exact same thing that Holly had done to get into trouble in the first place.

There was no turning back now. I gunned the motor and headed out to sea in a ten-foot rubber boat, in the dark, with no lights. I was a pirate again, foolishly running at speed in the British Virgin Islands like I knew where I was. I followed the shoreline to my right as the truck driver had instructed until I came to the first big bay. The water was rough across the entrance, so I slowed down. I kept my head on a swivel, looking for other vessels that might run me down. No one was running about in the dark but me, which was a blessing.

I came to the second inlet and hung a right. The water calmed, and I slowed to a speed that just barely kept me on a plane. There was a grouping of boats ahead, and I aimed for them. All of them showed anchor lights except one. I had found *Another Adventure.* I pulled alongside her, tied off, and climbed aboard. Before I got a chance to check on anything, two young men came zooming over in their dinghies.

"That's not your boat, asshole," one of them yelled.

"Beat it, jerkoff," the other one said.

"This is Holly Freeman's boat," I said. "She's in the hospital. I just came from visiting her. She asked me to take care of things out here. Call her if you want. I've got her number if you need it."

"Who are you?"

"I'm Breeze," I said. "An old friend of hers. Trust me on that one."

"Hard to trust someone who boards our friend's boat in the dark with no running lights," the bigger one said. "You can see why we'd be suspicious."

I pulled my phone out of my pocket, found Holly's number, and handed it to him.

"Check it out," I said. "Ask her if it's okay for Breeze to be here."

He pulled his own phone out and compared the numbers.

"He's got the right number," he said to his buddy. "What do you think?"

"Why are you so late getting out here," the smaller one asked.

"Look, I flew here from North Carolina on short notice," I said. "I went to see Holly then I had to round up a boat, get it in the water, steal some gas, and here I am. Got here as fast as I could."

"Okay," he said. "We were just concerned."

"You weren't concerned enough to close up her hatches," I said. "I'm going to be here a day or two. I'll take care of things since you didn't."

"Get some lights for that dinghy," the bigger one said.

"Yeah, thanks."

Apparently satisfied that I was legit, they retreated back to their vessels. I was relieved. I was in no shape to fight them off, and I needed a place to sleep. I went below and turned on some lights, including the anchor light. I checked the battery bank, which was okay. I'd take a look at the actual batteries in the daylight. I grabbed a flashlight and went forward to the bow. She had the anchor chain snubbed off on a bow cleat. I released it and fed out the rest of the chain and fifty more feet of rope. I started digging around for chaffing gear. Down in the anchor locker, I found some old fire hose that I'd given her many years ago. I laid it under the rope in the bow roller and tied it off with some string. I remembered giving her that hose one day in Andros. The night before she had anchored on the banks in a big storm. Her anchor rode broke while she and her crew slept. They didn't even realize it until they went to retrieve the anchor in the morning. Thankfully, they were many miles from any point of land. They drifted harmlessly instead of hitting a reef or running aground.

Lots of Holly memories flooded back into my mind. We had shared so much over the years, most of it good. We'd seen more adventure than most will see in a lifetime. We'd had our close calls too. We were trying to get this very boat from Grand Cayman back to Florida when a wicked storm snapped her mast. A piece of rigging slashed a big gash in my back. I lost a lot of blood, but Holly got me to the hospital in Marathon before it was too late. The wound later got infected, and I was nursed by a large, black Bahamian woman on Great Harbor Cay.

We traveled together on my boat all through the Bahamas. Later we returned with both boats and made it all the way to Luperon in the Dominican Republic. That's where we first parted ways, only to reunite later back in Florida. The cruising community is a small world. We made our mark on it both individually and as a couple. Now I was a landlubber while she was still out there doing it. Considering her predicament, I was almost glad to be a dirt dweller these days, although I did miss the sea.

I closed and dogged down her port lights before looking to see what she might have to eat onboard. It was slim pickings. I kept digging until I found the canned goods stash. Amongst the soup and vegetables, I found several cans of Dinty Moore Beef Stew. I'd loaded her up with that and Dinty's chicken and dumplings the last time I'd seen her in person, about three years earlier. They were well past their sell-by date, but I figured it was still good. I dug around for a can opener and a clean pan to warm it in. I'd eaten this crap a thousand times when I was broke. It was heavy on salt and preservatives, but it stuck to the ribs well enough.

I longed for a beer to wash it down with, but there were no beers in the fridge. I poked around looking for a bottle of rum or any kind of booze, but found nothing. Holly had given up the hooch. I went out on deck and took a quick survey. She had a five-gallon gas can about half full, which would come in handy. A handful of loose items were scattered here and there. I took them down below in case a storm blew up. Her diesel jugs were empty.

The beef stew was nowhere near as edible as I'd remembered it. I dumped the last of it overboard and rinsed out the pan with saltwater. As I put it in the sink, I looked around inside the boat. It wasn't particularly neat or clean. I had nothing else to do with my time, so I started straightening up. There was a drawer under the chart table that I wanted to put a few things in. When I opened it the first thing I saw was a note that I had written her before we left Luperon. It was a goodbye letter. I followed her out of the harbor's channel and stayed behind her for a while before veering off and setting a course back to Florida. There was a moment there where I didn't know what to do. I sat alone out in the ocean with three choices. I could stay with Holly, return to Luperon and spend my life with an old lover from my past, or go it alone. I chose the solitude of self. I was the one person that I could count on no matter what. Holly and I were never going to make it long-term. That pretty woman who wanted me in Luperon had never been able to hold me. There was no reason not to choose either, other than keeping my autonomy. That was all before I'd met Brody. She changed my calculations. She chose me even though I wasn't the wisest choice. She gave up her previous life to be with me in the world that I had chosen. Once I knew that she was truly the one for me, I gave up that life to please her.

Those thoughts made me miss Brody badly. We were seldom apart, but now I was half a world away, coming to the rescue of an old love. I could not bring myself to regret the decision to help Holly, but suddenly I wanted to be done with it and go back home.

# Six

I couldn't sleep that night. There was not one drop of alcohol to drink, and I was in a strange place. A log cabin in the woods had become a true home for me. Brody and Red were my life these days, not messing about in boats. I had made my peace about leaving the cruising life behind. Now, lying awake on Holly's boat, I started to think about it again. There were constant chores to manage when you live on a boat. Maintenance and repair never seemed to end. Locating and hauling fresh water was a constant struggle. Every supply had to be carried across the water in a dinghy, or a dock had to be located and paid for. Trash had to be disposed of. Wind and waves could ruin your day. Thunderstorms were a threat to life and property. Bugs could make you miserable, even in paradise.

No, I couldn't see myself going back. I'd come to enjoy the simple pleasures, like turning on a faucet and having unlimited water or taking long hot showers. Storms didn't bother me anymore. My house wouldn't drag its anchor and run aground. I was happy living on land, as happy as I'd ever been. This was only a temporary situation. I needed to be here to help a friend. As soon as she was able to fend for herself, I'd run back home as fast as possible.

I took some cushions out on deck and tried to get comfortable while watching the stars. I dozed briefly from time to time, but never really did experience any deep sleep. The rising sun put a stop to that. Holly had no bacon or eggs or anything much else to eat for breakfast. I took the newly acquired dinghy to the Nanny Cay Resort to see if I could get some grub. I found a laid-back establishment that didn't care that I'd arrived by dinghy or that I hadn't showered in two days, but no breakfast. I soon learned that several places would open for lunch at eleven. Island folk are not early risers. I found myself at Peg Leg's, where I ordered a Mahi sandwich and a

Caribe beer. It was early for beer, but I was alcohol deficient. It was cold and tasty, so I had another. I felt ready to tackle the world after two beers and a fish sandwich, so I headed back to *Another Adventure* to see what needed to be done.

I checked the oil and anti-freeze as well as the belt tension. The battery fluid levels were fine. They looked brand new as a matter of fact. The battery compartment and the engine space were neat and clean. Holly was more concerned about the mechanics of her vessel than the aesthetics. I tidied up the cabin some more before readying myself for the ride back to Road Town Harbor and another trip to the hospital. I went directly to the closest store to buy locks and cable, so my stolen dinghy wouldn't get stolen again. I secured it well and went to the front of the Mooring compound to catch a cab. I got a new driver this time, but he was happy to take me to the hospital. It wasn't one of his regular stops.

"I mostly go back and forth from the airport," he told me. "This will be a nice change of pace."

"You want to come back for me in an hour, or is that too much trouble?"

"I'll wait at the Moorings," he said. "If I don't pick up a fare I'll be available. Pay both ways, though."

He handed me his number, and I stuck it in my pocket.

"Thanks," I said. "I'll try you when I'm done here."

I'd forgotten Holly's request for something decent to eat. I walked a few blocks north until I found Dove Restaurant. I paid forty-two bucks for an Angus beef dinner with sides. It was still warm when I returned to the hospital. The smell of it filled the elevator and made me hungry again. I carried it to Holly's room and presented it to her like a maître de.

"You are an angel," she said. "Don't mind me while I'm stuffing my face with this goodness."

"Your boat is secure," I said. "I put out a bunch more rode and started the engine today and backed down on your anchor. She's stuck good."

"It's not a bad spot to be in," she said. "I should be out of here in a day or two."

"Some of your neighbors gave me a hard time last night," I said. "But I was able to keep them from kicking my ass."

"Good intentions," she said. "Nice to know they were keeping an eye on things."

"What are the doctors telling you?"

"They refer to my collapsed lung as a pneumothorax," she said. "It might be two weeks until it resolves itself, but if no fluid collects, I can get this tube out and get out of here soon."

"You are going to have to be careful and take it easy for a while," I said. "Don't push it if you want things to heal properly."

"My frigging ribs bother me the most," she said. "Every movement is like a knife stabbing me."

"Remember when that shark busted my ribs?"

"You're lucky you weren't lunch," she said.

"I don't think they ever did heal properly," I said. "I reinjured them several times, even years later."

"Gee, that's good news," she said.

"You're young and strong," I said. "You'll be fine as long as you don't overdo it before they are healed."

"I need to get back to work," she said. "Climbing masts and diving bottoms."

"You're working down here?"

"In St. Thomas," she said. "For a charter company."

"Why?"

"I don't want to tell you."

"Do you need the money?" I asked. "What happened to what you made working with Tommy Thompson?"

"I blew some," she said. "Lost the rest. Long story."

"Easy come, easy go."

"What are you up to these days?" she asked.

"Brace yourself," I said. "Settled down with a wonderful woman. Living on land."

"No way in hell," she said. "Not Breeze."

"We have a log cabin in the mountains now," I said.

"With Brody?" she asked. "Where?"

"Blue Ridge Mountains in North Carolina."

"Holy crap," she said. "That's a long way from a boat in Florida. I would have never thought it."

"It's a good life," I said. "We started our own investigative business."

"Good for you if that's what you want," she said. "As long as you're happy."

"I am," I said. "We are. Right now, I'm worried about you."

"I hit some hard times before this happened," she said. "Now it's going to be doubly hard."

"I noticed you had no food onboard," I said. "How bad is it?"

"I'm catching fish mostly," she said. "I've got an emergency fund, but this nonsense will likely deplete it."

"Once you're back to work, will you make enough to get by?"

"More than enough," she said. "But things will be tight until I start getting paid again."

"It will work out," I said. "Shit always works out."

"Shit works out," she said. "The best advice you've ever given me. I tell myself that all the time."

"Eat your dinner," I said. "I want to get back before dark."

"Good idea," she said. "Thanks for this. Thanks for everything."

"You're going to be just fine."

I got another cab ride back to the harbor, but before taking off, I stopped in the small grocery that serviced the charter customers. I got a six-pack of beer and a pound of shrimp for dinner. Eggs and bacon were purchased for breakfast. Lunch meat and bread along with a few condiments went in the basket for lunches. The only thing missing was liquor. I wasn't sure where to buy booze. I couldn't leave my supplies in the dinghy unguarded either. On my way down the dock, I kept an eye out for partiers. When I found a group drinking mixed drinks, I asked to buy a bottle of whatever they had.

"This is the good stuff, man," someone told me. "Can't part with any of it, but I've got a bottle of cheap rum you can have."

I held out a twenty.

"Will this cover it?" I asked.

"Twice what it's worth but I'll take it anyway," he said.

"I don't have a problem with that," I said. "Where did you get your booze?"

"You have to take a taxi," he said. "Adds twenty dollars to your bill."

"Every cab ride is twenty bucks down here," I said. "Doesn't matter where."

I got my bottle of booze and started the boat ride back to Nanny Cay. I should have given myself more time to look for lights for the little boat, but if I hurried, I wouldn't need them. I topped off the gas tank from Holly's can and fired up the motor. It started easily and idled smoothly. It was a good buy and would service Holly well. Once clear of the docks I hauled ass out of there and kept the throttle on full until I got back to *Another Adventure*. I tied off and unloaded my goodies. My second night down here would be much better than the first.

I popped open a beer and put the rest in the fridge, along with the shrimp. I sat on deck and watched as other cruisers returned from their day on the island. The guys who had tried to run me off went by, and I gave them a wave. From where the boat was anchored, the sunset occurred over land. I sat and watched it go down before attempting to start dinner. It reminded me of the old days when I watched the sunset every night. We didn't have a view of it from our cabin. I missed that.

The one and only seasoning to use for steamed shrimp is Old Bay. Holly did not stock it. I dug and dug until I found some kind of Cajun seafood seasoning. It would have to do. She did not have a proper steamer either, so I had to boil the shrimp with the Cajun stuff. The end result wasn't bad. I ate my fill along with a little bread. I cleaned up my mess and put everything back where I'd found it.

I carried the cheap rum back out on deck. I didn't find any shot glasses, so I drank right out of the bottle. It tasted awful and burned on the way down, but that didn't deter me much. My mind worked a mile a minute, and I needed to slow it down if I was ever going to sleep. I was in a position to fully see just how important Brody was to me. After thousands of nights alone on a boat, being with her every night was more than a welcome change. Any romantic feelings that I'd had for Holly were well in the past. I was still her friend, here to render aid and assistance, but there was zero chance of future involvement. Those simple truths were very clear to me that night under the stars, anchored in the British Virgin Islands. I managed to choke down enough of the rotgut rum to fall asleep and stay under until dawn.

The next day was spent loading up with groceries to fill Holly's larder. I managed to also acquire some navigation lights for the dinghy and refill her five-gallon gas can as well as the dinghy's tank. I'd bought enough food to last her several weeks, but no fresh vegetables or fruit. I didn't eat that stuff, and I didn't want it to spoil waiting for her to get out of the hospital. I went to visit her during the evening hours, now that I had lights. I brought a good old fashioned cheeseburger for her. It wasn't hot, but she devoured it in short order.

"They're going to test my lung capacity tomorrow," she said. "If I pass, I can be set free."

"Any idea what all this is going to cost?"

"None," she said. "I won't be able to come back here and get hurt."

"I'll help you get the boat back to St. Thomas," I said. "I can catch a flight from there. It will save me the puddle jumper ride from here."

"You're the best, Breeze," she said. "You didn't have to do any of this."

"I wanted to," I said. "But this will be the end of it. I'm going back to Brody with a new appreciation."

"How so?"

"Sitting out there on your boat," I said. "I still get it, but I can live without it now. It's not home for me anymore."

"I won't ever leave the water," she said. "Land sucks."

"I thought the same for a long time," I said. "Never say never."

"I don't know," she said. "If that one special guy came along, maybe I could think about it, but not anytime soon."

"You'll know they're special when all you want to do is make them happy," I said. "I didn't have to move to land. I could have stayed out here forever, and Brody would have come along with me, but her happiness became more important than mine."

"I've never experienced that," she said.

"Stay open to the possibility," I said. "Grab it when it comes along."

"I've been a hard-headed fool more than once," she admitted. "And so have you."

"I can still be a dumbass," I said. "I just try to keep it to a minimum."

"You sound like a wise older sage," she said. "But maybe that's what you've always been to me."

"I will always cherish when our lives were intertwined," I said. "It was a good time for both of us."

"But we've both moved on," she said. "For real this time."

I went to her bed and leaned in to give her a gentle hug. She kissed my neck before pushing me away. She held her hand out between us before zipping her lip with it.

"No more talk," she said.

"I'm going to talk with the staff before I go," I said. "Get the scoop on your outlook. I'll be back tomorrow. Anything you need?"

"Find me a clean pair of shorts and a shirt of some kind," she said. "The stuff I was wearing when they brought me in is pretty trashed."

"Will do," I said. "Good night, girl."

I was able to track down her attending physician. After asking about her condition and prognosis, I inquired about the cost of her care. He couldn't really answer me but was willing to attempt to find out. A nurse directed us to an administrator. The doc defined what had been done and what resources had been used.

"I won't be able to give you an exact amount," she said. "There are too many ancillary charges to be added."

"You mean like the fifty dollar aspirin and the thousand dollar saline bags?"

"I'd need a complete accounting from the rest of the staff," she said.

"Let me tell you something," I said. "That girl in there has no money. I'm your only shot at collecting anything. I want to be fair, but I need you to be fair with me. She can walk out of here, and you'll never see a dime, or you can make a deal with me right now."

"Give him a nice round figure," the doctor said. "Something reasonable."

"If insurance were involved we'd be looking at thirty grand," the admin lady said.

"It's not," I said. "I'll be trying to get cash tomorrow. Make it possible that I can get enough to settle this score. It's all you're going to get."

"Okay, five grand," she said.

"Done," I said. "I'll see you in the morning. And thank you."

"Thank you, mister?"

"Breeze," I said. "Mister Breeze."

I walked out of there humming a Lynyrd Skynyrd song.

*Call me the Breeze*
*I keep blowin' down the road*
*Well now, they call me the Breeze*
*I keep blowin' down the road.*

# SEVEN

I still had half a bottle of rum left, but it really did taste like shit, so I got a ride to a real liquor store and got some of the good stuff. The whiskey selection in the BVI is poor, but they do have plenty of fine rums available. My chore list was finished, as far as I was concerned. All I was waiting for was Holly's release. I guessed that my final offer to pay her bill would hasten their decision to let her out of the hospital. They knew they couldn't milk her for any more money.

I spent the evening out on deck with my bottle and my thoughts. I would see this mission through, but I couldn't wait to get home. This trip had reaffirmed my commitment not only to Brody but to life on land. It was nice that I was in a position to come to Holly's rescue, but this would clearly be the final time. She was my last connection to life at sea. Even though I didn't think of her often, I knew she was out there somewhere, still living the life I had once enjoyed.

The first thing I planned to do once we reached St. Thomas was to call Brody and check in. The second would be to arrange a flight home. I wanted to sit on the porch and listen to the creek sing its mountain song. I wanted to throw a Frisbee for Red to fetch. Mostly, I wanted to see that sparkle in Brody's eyes and know that she loved me as much as I loved her. The rum made these urges worse but eventually made me sleepy enough to push it all out of my mind. I stumbled below and went to bed. The pillow smelled like Holly.

I dreamt of the Moon-eyed People. They were carrying rocks up the hill alongside the New River. I could walk among them without being noticed. They stacked the rocks one by one on the wall they were building on top of the rise. I couldn't tell what the purpose of this exercise was. They placed their rock and returned to the river to gather another one. They didn't speak to each other or to me. The moon was up, and these creatures shined like glow sticks as they moved back and forth. They were so blindingly white that I couldn't make out their features, other than the oversized eyes. Then it was morning, and I was awake. The rising sun blinded me as it peeked in a port light. I should have slept wearing sunglasses.

I shook off the dream and got up to face the day. There was no coffee. I could have bought some, but I didn't find a coffee maker on the boat. I drank water while I prepared my breakfast. I had some juice with my bacon and eggs. I wanted toast but couldn't find a toaster either. Holly obviously lived like a barbarian, with no booze and no coffee or toast. Booze and coffee were the building blocks of life. They weren't luxuries; they were necessities.

I cleaned up after my meal, and then I cleaned myself up. I managed a cold water shave and a GI shower with a washcloth and a sink. I put on clean clothes and even slapped on a little aftershave. It would cover any body odor that I'd missed with the rag. I threw a hat on over my still dirty hair and looked in the mirror. Some old dude looked back at me. He had the wrinkles that a mariner gets after years on the ocean. He was somewhat leathery after his time in the Florida sun. He'd gone mostly gray, but if you asked him, he'd tell you his hair was blonde. At least he still had his hair. I wished the stranger in the mirror a good day.

As I climbed down into the dinghy, I noticed that my joints were less achy down here in the Caribbean warmth. My knees didn't moan, and my back wasn't complaining either. I wondered if the mountain altitude made arthritis worse, or if it had just been the cold. It was clear, though, that here at sea level in warm temperatures my body felt better, younger even. *Enjoy it while you can, Breeze.*

So, I was chipper and feeling sporty as I drove the little dink back to the harbor so I could hopefully break Holly out of hospital jail. The wind was in my hair, and there was the smell of salt in the air. It felt good to buzz along at speed and take it all in. I had a little extra pep in my step when I got to the hospital. The staff greeted me warmly. Everyone was friendly, except Holly. Even though she'd been given her release, she was in a foul mood. She had suddenly realized that her diminished condition was going to be a severe handicap on a boat. She blamed fate, the Gods, the man who ran her over, and anyone else she could think of. She responded to inspirational platitudes with a big fuck you. She was mad at the Universe.

I had the misfortune of being the one person that she knew at this point in time. I was there to help, but she wasn't grateful at all. I didn't want to screw up her release, so I let it roll off my back until we were out of that place and on our way to the dinghy.

"You might want to check that attitude," I said. "It doesn't become you."

"Fucking landlubber," she said.

"Whoa, girl," I said. "Check back with me in about ten years when you have as much experience as I have. I'm way out of my way helping you down here. Show a little respect."

"Everybody is telling me it's going to be okay," she said. "My life is good and screwed, but hey, it's all good. I'm a badass, and I can handle it. I'm the strongest woman they've ever known. Blah, blah, blah."

"Are those things not true?"

"I'm hurt bad, Breeze," she said. "I'm weak and broke and soon to be starving. Can I just wallow in my misery for a bit? Is that too much to ask?"

"This is the life you chose," I said. "One with no security and no health insurance. You've had a real setback, but something tells me you'll recover."

"How would you know?" she said, practically spitting at me. "I'm still out here while you live amongst the dirt people. How am I going to recover, exactly?"

My good mood had been shattered by her pity party. I didn't want to make her any madder, but I did want her to appreciate what I'd done for her.

"Listen up, little miss bitchy pants," I said. "I paid your hospital bill. You're free and clear of that debt. I also loaded your boat with a ton of food. I'm about to help you get back to St. Thomas. My airfare was ridiculously expensive, as will my return airfare be. I'm going to be out about ten grand when this is over. What will you be out? A few weeks of pay from missing work? I'll give you that too if it makes you shut the hell up. Meanwhile, you don't owe me a damn thing. That's how much you mean to me, but if you keep this whining up, then we're done. I'll find my own way to St. Thomas. You can figure out how to solo sail your boat with broken ribs and a punctured lung. You up for that?"

"I can't do it," she said. "I won't be able to do it for a while, but I need to get back there."

"I'll help," I said. "If you shut up and realize that you're lucky to be alive."

She didn't respond to that. She didn't say a word all the way back to her boat. When we got there, getting her up on deck was a chore. She couldn't climb with her arms, and any attempt to help her caused pain. A sailboat was not the place for her to be in her condition. She sat and stared at her feet. I noticed some blood on the front of her shirt. It was coming from where the chest tube had been.

"First aid stuff?" I asked.

"In the head cabinet."

I got peroxide, alcohol wipes, and anti-bacterial cream out of the kit. She was lying down when I returned. I lifted her shirt to examine the wound. She reflexively tried to pull it back down.

"Not the first time I've seen your boobs," I said. "Chill out. Let me clean this and put a new bandage on it."

The hole was oozing some nasty looking goop, which I wiped off with the alcohol swabs. I poured peroxide over it several times, cleaning it each time. When the fizzing lessened enough, I put the cream over it and taped a new bandage on the area.

"How's your breathing?" I asked. "Are you getting enough air?"

"As long as I'm not moving," she said. "Getting onboard about killed me."

"Keep that in mind," I said. "When you get anxious to do too much."

"I am so fucked."

"What's your situation over there?" I asked.

"I've been working for a charter company," she said. "I do the shit jobs that no one else wants to do. I climb, I dive, I fit my bendy ass in tight engine compartments. I can't do any of that."

"You'll be back at it soon enough," I said. "But in the meantime, can those people help you?"

"I just don't know, man," she said. "They're friendly enough, but when it comes right down to it, we're not really friends."

"Maybe somebody there is," I said. "Someone will step up."

"Remains to be seen," she said. "They might let me lay there and die for all I know."

I was getting fed up with her negativity. It wouldn't help matters as she recovered. I wanted to give her a good slap and tell her off, but I doubted that was what she needed at that moment. Still, I had to be firm. I couldn't be there to hold her hand much longer.

"You've been through some rough patches before," I said. "You survived and came out of it stronger than ever. You wouldn't be out here if that weren't true. I'm not going to sugar coat it. This is a bad one. You need rest and plenty of it. Those ribs are going to hurt for months, if not longer. You'll need resolve, and you'll need to focus on getting better and not losing it while you heal. You're going to have to depend on the kindness of others. Pissing them off with your shitty attitude is not the way to do it. Humble yourself and let people know that you need help. You'll get it, as long as you allow it and appreciate it. You'll be in a position to repay them someday. Don't forget what they did for you. Finally, always remember this; shit works out."

"I should have known that was coming," she said. "It's just hard to see it right now."

"You told me it was the best advice I've ever given you," I said. "Don't go forgetting it now."

"Point taken," she said. "But I'm still feeling bitchy. Can you help me below so I can go to bed?"

I went below first and had her turn around to descend the steps backward. She kept her hands on the grab rail and very slowly came down into the salon. I held her arm and directed her to her bunk. Getting in it involved a slight hop up. I stopped her and went to look for something to act as a step. I found a box containing some engine parts and put it at the foot of her bed. She used it successfully to climb up and lie down.

"Become Sleeping Beauty," I said. "I'll kiss you when it's time to wake up."

"Please don't," she said. "I haven't brushed my teeth in a while."

"Thanks for the warning," I said. "See you tomorrow."

She was out of it before I got back on deck. I was again alone on a boat in the Caribbean. There was nothing left to do but kill the good bottle of rum. I didn't even fix dinner. I sat on deck with my bottle and tried to count the stars. I lost track at a million, or a thousand, I'm not sure which. At some point, I fell asleep right where I sat. The sun woke me, reflecting off the empty rum bottle directly into my face. I felt like my tongue needed a shave. I went below and splashed some water on my face before looking in on my patient. She was still asleep. There was a stain on her shirt, indicating that liquid was oozing through. I let her sleep, knowing that the smell of cooking bacon would bring her to life.

It worked much better than any kiss from a prince would, and I was no prince. She appeared in the galley, hair a mess.

"I'm leaking again," she said.

"Let me finish here, and I'll take care of it."

"I can probably see it in the mirror," she said.

"Knock yourself out," I said.

I flipped the bacon and got the last few eggs out of the fridge. Holly called me from the head.

"You've got to see this," she said.

"What am I looking at?"

"This scar looks exactly like an anchor," she said. "Do you see it?"

"No doubt about it," I said. "Your surgeon had to do that on purpose."

"No way this was an accident," she said. "Pretty freaking cool if you ask me."

"A true badge of honor," I said. "It will make for great bar stories someday."

"Hand me the first aid stuff," she said. "I can handle this. I'll need to do it by myself once you leave anyway."

"Here you go," I said. "Yell if you need me."

I scrambled the eggs and made two plates. Holly appeared a few minutes later with a fresh bandage and a bikini top on. We sat and ate without talking much. I started to clean up, but she took over the job, so I went out on deck to chill. It was a perfect day to set sail for St. Thomas, but I didn't know if the patient was up to it. It was her boat, and it was up to her when she wanted to travel. It was thirty minutes or more before she came out and joined me in the sun.

"I'm a bit torn on what to do with you," she said.

"With me?" I asked. "It's you that you should be concerned about."

"My first instinct is to get you out of here as soon as possible," she said. "I hate being dependent on anyone, especially you, but…"

"But what?"

"I like having you here," she said. "You're probably the best friend I've ever had. I get the feeling this will be the last time I ever see you. The real last time, now that you live on land. Now that you are settled down with Brody."

"You're not having any romantic notions about this, are you?"

"No offense but I don't see you that way anymore," she said. "Not like a dad either even though you've taken care of me."

"So we can end it as friends?"

"Friends," she said. "I will be sad when you leave."

"I have to go soon," I said. "This isn't my life anymore."

"But you put everything on hold to fly down here to help me," she said. "That means a lot to me. I won't forget it."

"If you ever get to western North Carolina you are welcome to pay us a visit," I said.

"How close are you to the Appalachian Trail?"

"Minutes," I said. "You thinking about hiking it?"

"Maybe someday," she said. "Before I get too old."

"I'm already too old," I told her. "I've developed bad knees."

"Could have fooled me," she said. "You look as spry as ever."

"Funny, they haven't bothered me since I got here," I said. "And I've been busy."

"Maybe the mountains are bad for you," she said with a grin.

"You think I should sell everything and buy a boat?"

"Whatever makes you happy," she said. "But first we need to get you home."

"Ready when you are."

"Can you sail this bad boy without much help from me?" she asked.

"You were my teacher," I said. "I learned from the best."

"We can motor out of here," she said. "Sail across, then motor into the marina."

"Sounds like a plan."

It wasn't a long trip; you could practically see St. Thomas from where we were. It had been a while since I'd sailed, but I knew the basics. Holly fired up the diesel and instructed me to remove the mainsail cover. I went to the bow and waited for her to be ready before raising the anchor. The engine warmed up, the anchor was pulled, and we were underway. I went back to the helm and stood next to

Holly. She worked the wheel with one arm, letting her weak one dangle at her side.

"Those sheets right there," she said. "Raise her up all the way as quickly as you can. Wait until I'm into the wind."

We nosed out into the Sir Francis Drake Channel, and she gave me the order. I hauled on the lines and watched the sail go up smoothly. Holly killed the engine as soon as we caught the wind. We started sailing west toward St. John. We passed by that island to the north and set a course for Vessup Bay and Red Hook. A slip was waiting for her at American Yacht Harbor. There is a bit of open water between St. John and St. Thomas, not much, but enough to let me remember what it was like to be out on the sea. *Another Adventure* sliced the waves under wind power. The only sound was from her hull cutting through the waves. We were traveling as fast as I ever had in my trawler with just the mainsail. We could have gone faster with the addition of a jib, but we didn't need it. The sailing was smooth and leisurely, which I figured was all Holly needed. She could go out and run herself ragged once she healed properly. I'd be looking for trout in the creek when that happened.

It was over too soon. I lowered the sail as we entered the bay. Holly steered us towards the dock under power. She was damn good with her vessel. We got into the slip and secured without a hitch. Once she was satisfied with the lines, she begged off and went to lie down. I was left to explain to the dockmaster what I knew of the situation. He said he would relay the information to Holly's boss. I followed him to the office so I could prepay a month's worth of slip rent for her.

"Think she'll be ready to work in a month?" he asked.

"That's up to her," I said. "But at least you know the rent is paid."

"You must be a good friend, mister," he said.

"I do what I can."

I almost gave him my number in case there was trouble in the future, but I didn't. This really was going to be the end of it for Holly and me. The chances that she'd have another accident like this one were slim. The chances that she'd call me again were also slim. The chances that I'd travel half-way around the world to rescue her again were next to nothing. The dockmaster didn't need my number.

# EIGHT

I wanted a beer, so I went to the bar on premises called Island Time Pub. I left a note for Holly to meet me there. It was a pizza and wings place, which was fine with me. I decided to wait for Holly before ordering food. I sat and drank beer until she showed up. She had showered and put on her Sunday best. Her hair was somewhat managed. She smelled good. It was nice to feel all eyes upon us when she sat next to me.

"I would like to buy you a beer," I said. "If you haven't sworn off alcohol entirely."

"Mostly it's an unnecessary expense," she said. "I'm all in if you're buying."

"Two Red Stripes," I said to the barkeep. "Keep them coming."

"You got it," the bartender said.

"You want pizza?" I asked Holly.

"Sure," she said. "I'm starving."

We ate pizza and drank beer for a couple of hours. There were a few pieces left, so Holly took them to go.

"I love cold pizza for breakfast," she said.

"I prefer to warm it up."

"Well, there you go," she said. "This is why we can't be together. We're leftover pizza opposites."

"You're right," I said. "It would never work."

"I'm envious of Brody, you know," she said.

"As in jealous?"

"No, it's not that," she said. "Just that you found the right person to be with forever. I worry that will never happen for me."

"You've got a lot to offer," I said. "But your lifestyle automatically rules out most men."

"I can't give it up," she said. "Not even for love. I'm going to have to find it out here or not at all."

"I wish you the best," I said.

"Are you leaving tomorrow?"

"I need to check on flights, but probably," I said. "Unless there's some reason I need to stay."

"Maybe we've grown up enough to say a proper goodbye this time."

"I hate goodbyes," I said. "As you know, I pretty much suck at saying goodbye."

"You did the right thing down in Luperon," she said. "I sort of knew it was coming. Saved us both some agony."

"I'm glad you see it that way," I said. "I felt guilty about it for a long time."

"You're off the hook," she said. "How do you want to spend your last hours here?"

"A decent bottle of rum would do nicely."

"Stonehouse Cellars is up the street," she said. "They've got a cool glass elevator we can ride."

"Lead the way."

We sat on the boat, drank rum, and remembered the old days when we were a team. We got into so much shit together that I'd forgotten some of it. Our first shared mission was capturing a guy named Tom Melendez, who had hidden himself away in the Bahamas. We ended up helping him escape the mobsters that had paid us to find him. That little episode seemed to have happened a hundred years ago. A lot of water had passed under our keels since then. We had tried to be lovers. We had given it a good shot, trying to understand exactly what love was supposed to be. We did it on our own terms, island hopping and avoiding the world. In the end, we each decided that we didn't have whatever it takes, not together anyway.

We remained friends, occasionally sharing a bed, but by then we knew that nothing between us was permanent. She came in and out of my life like a summer storm after that. I chose to only recall the good times. Holly was a sunny person; always upbeat and willing to help anyone. Right now, she was down, but I knew what was inside of her. She'd be off on *Another Adventure* as soon as possible, spreading goodwill across the Caribbean Sea.

She asked me to lay with her that night, not to make love, but just to hold each other. In a moment of weakness, I agreed. I did not let that weakness drive me to do anything that I would later regret. I held her softly until we both fell asleep. We were still embraced when I woke up in the middle of the night. I had to pee, so I wriggled out of her arms and spent the rest of the night on the settee by myself. All I could think about was getting home to Brody.

I reserved an early flight as soon as I woke up. I called Brody with the news and arrival time. It was good to hear her voice.

"Everything is fine," I told her. "I can't wait to get home."

"Red keeps looking for you," she said. "I miss you too."

"On my way," I said.

The Cyril E. King International Airport was on the opposite side of the island. I needed to get moving, but Holly was still asleep. The mature, adult thing to do involved waking her up for a proper goodbye. We practically promised each other that we'd finally get it right. That's not what I decided to do. I called for a shuttle to the airport and walked out of the marina to meet the driver on the street. A van soon pulled up to get me.

"Go, driver," I said. "Take me to the airport."

I was gone, probably forever.

There was nothing to see for most of the flight but the open ocean. That big blue sea would remain Holly's home, while I continued to make a life in the mountains. As we flew over the coast of South Carolina, the sight of land closed the door on my old life for good. I can't say that I didn't enjoy the brief visit to the islands. It was nice to sit on a boat and look out over the water. The warmth was divine; seeming to cure the aches in my old bones. It had been good to visit with Holly too, despite her negative attitude. I did see a glimmer of hope in her during our last night together. I told myself not to look back. *Boats and blondes are behind you, Breeze.*

Brody was waiting for me with a big smile and a twinkle in her eye. It was exactly what I needed to see. We shared a prolonged hug there on the concourse, before heading to the car. I filled her in during the two-hour drive to the cabin.

"She's roughed up pretty badly," I said. "Won't be able to work for a while, even though she's broke."

"That's a shame," Brody said. "Both that she's hurt and has no money. What happened to her gold earnings?"

"Gone, but I didn't press her about it," I said. "She was in a foul enough mood as it was."

"Any of the old attraction come back to you?"

"We still care for each other," I said. "But neither of us attempted to rekindle that dead flame."

"You're a good friend to her," she said.

"That's going to be the last time," I said. "I dropped a ton of cash to bail her out and get her through the next month. I bought her a new dinghy, paid slip rent, and settled the hospital bill."

"Don't write her off on my account."

"I'm not writing her off," I said. "But I can't do that again. I can't always be there for her when she gets in trouble. We have our new life together, and that's what I want to focus on."

"How did you end it?"

"I left without saying goodbye, again," I said. "Slipped away while she was sleeping."

"Damn, Breeze."

"Goodbyes are too hard," I said. "Especially ones with finality."

"Welcome back to land," she said. "How was it out on the water?"

"I enjoyed that part of it," I said. "My joints felt better. The heat felt good. I stayed busy and took care of business."

"Maybe we can plan a vacation to some tropical location," she said. "Recharge your batteries now and then."

"Sure, but it's almost summer here now," I said. "Let's see how a mountain summer goes. We can fly to Aruba when it's cold and snowy here."

"That's one place we haven't been to."

"Look it up," I suggested. "See if it will suit us."

We drove up Pigeon Roost Road, then down the gravel of McGuire Mountain Road to our cabin. Brody warned me about Red before I got out of the car.

"He's been a mess," she said. "All he does is look out the windows and scratch the doors. I take him outside, but he doesn't need to go. He's looking for you."

"Grab my bag," I said. "I'll give him a proper, hello."

My hound dog burst out the door as soon as I opened it. He jumped up on me, spun in a few circles, jumped again, and licked my face. I got on the ground and hugged him and rubbed his ears, but he kept wiggling loose and jumping around. He gave me a yelp before finally settling down enough for me to pet him. I had slobber on half my face, mixed with a little fur.

"That's my good boy," I told him. "I'm sorry, buddy. I won't stay gone again for long."

"He is getting more attention than I am," Brody said. "A man and his dog."

"I can fix that," I said. "But I need to shower first."

"Yes," she said. "Yes, you do."

It felt like I was washing the salt not only off my skin but out of my soul. I got a taste of my old life, and I enjoyed it, but it did not make me want to return. After showering, I went out on the porch in my boxers with a towel around my neck. I breathed in the clean mountain air and listened to the song of the creek. This was home now. My life was here with Brody, of that there was no doubt. Brody joined me, stripped down to her lacey underthings. We were soon testing the springs on our porch futon. It was as good as any sex I'd ever had on the deck of my boat.

"Your little trip to the islands didn't make you homesick?"

"For the water or the mountains?" I asked.

"For your old boat," she responded. "Your old way of life."

"I gave it some serious thought," I said. "I decided that I'd rather be here. There was a time when that would have been impossible to imagine."

"That day when you told me you wanted to buy a cabin in the woods shocked the shit out of me," she said. "But I've got to tell you; I'm very happy here."

"Me too, baby," I said. "Me too."

# NINE

We received a strange phone call a few days later. It was from the Charlotte Area Paranormal Society or CAPS. Our friend Loon had called them about the Moon-eyed People on the New River. They wanted us to guide them to the place where mushroom boy had claimed to see them. I'm not much of a believer in ghost hunters and paranormal phenomenon, so I didn't commit. I told them I'd think about it and get back to them. I also informed them that our time wasn't free. We weren't in the business of donating our time, especially for something not related to law enforcement.

As soon as I hung up, Brody got on the computer to check them out. Their website claimed they used all sorts of scientific technology for their investigations, like thermal imaging, digital audio recorders that could detect electronic voice phenomena, full spectrum photography, video recorders, and electromagnetic field detectors. It all sounded like bunk to me. We went back through their archives looking for any solid evidence that they'd discovered in the past. The only thing that came close was a video of the Brown Mountain Lights. That got my attention, but it didn't seem like a paranormal issue to me.

I sat on my decision until they called us a second time, offering a thousand bucks for one day's work. All they wanted was for me to lead them into the wilderness and show them the rock wall and where these little people had been seen. I explained that we had taken canoes down the river to get to the camping area and that we had walked a good way to the spot in question. They weren't deterred. I pointed out that there were no facilities, just a place to pitch a tent. That didn't bother them either.

"Just lead the way," the lady said. "We'll do whatever it takes."

I tried to remember the conditions on the night our mushroom eater had freaked out.

The sky was clear, the moon was shining, but it wasn't full. The weather had been stable for days. I suggested they pick a day that mirrored those conditions.

"Round up some canoes and call me when you're ready," I said.

"Can't we take a small boat?" she asked.

"Too shallow for anything but canoes or kayaks," I explained. "Hard to carry gear on a kayak."

"I understand," she said. "How remote is this place?"

"It's in a state park," I told her. "You can drive on the blacktop to the lower parking lot where the canoe launch is located. Paddle a mile or two and beach the canoes. Set up camp then hike to the spot."

"Sounds a little rugged," she said.

"You said you'd do whatever it takes," I said. "I'll show you where it allegedly happened."

"You seem skeptical," she said.

"Extremely."

"How many people witnessed this event?" she asked.

"One guy tripping on mushrooms, or worse," I answered. "It's a thin thread you're pulling."

"We've heard other reports from different locations," she said. "The legend is well-rooted in your part of the state and all the way down to Murphy."

"We saw the sculpture at the museum there," I said. "It almost made the myth seem possible."

"We don't need you to be a believer," she said. "We just need a guide."

"For a thousand bucks I'll take you anywhere you want to go," I said. "But I might want to stick around and watch what you people do."

"You're more than welcome," she said. "We might surprise you."

"I made a promise recently to be more open-minded about this sort of thing," I explained. "That's why I'm agreeing to help."

"Excellent," she said. "Let me check with my team, and I'll get back to you."

Brody was conflicted about our new mission. She was thrilled that I wanted to participate, but not much looking forward to spending the night in the woods. I offered to go alone, but she wouldn't allow it.

"I prodded you into just this type of thing," she said. "I can't make you do it by yourself."

"I agreed due to your prodding," I said. "I thought I was doing what you wanted."

"You were," she said. "That's why I have to go with you."

"It's just one night," I said. "Red won't even miss us."

"We should take him with us," she said. "I'd feel better having him along."

"You going to let him sleep with us?"

"Didn't think of that," she said. "Can we get him his own shelter?"

"A pup tent?" I asked, laughing out loud. "Hey, Red, you want a pup tent?"

My hound dog cocked his head sideways, trying to understand what I was asking him. He loved the woods. I'd be happy to take him with us; I just needed to find a little doggie-sized tent for him. Should I buy him his own sleeping bag too?

Within the week, the weather and the moon phase looked right to go hunting the little people. All the arrangements were made to meet up with the CAPS crew at the lower parking lot in the New River State Park. Brody and I brought enough in the way of supplies to make ourselves comfortable. The ghost hunters brought lots of equipment and little else. They planned to stay awake all night long, so they didn't bring tents or sleeping bags. They filled two canoes with people and gear anyway. Brody and I teamed up to portage our canoe to the launch area. Our customers used one of the campground wagons to wheel their two vessels. It was an awkward operation. We beat them to the launch by fifteen minutes. We had the rest of our stuff in backpacks.

Red was well-behaved, but he knew something special was up. He kept his ears perked and looked around constantly. I prayed he didn't see a squirrel or a rabbit and run off after it. He wasn't sure about getting into the canoe, but I managed to coax him aboard. He took a position on the bow so that he could see where we were going. As soon as the rest of the crew were ready, we began our paddle up the river. Instead of stopping at the same place we'd camped before, we continued on to get closer to the rock wall and the supposed home of the Moon-eyes. It didn't matter where we camped; there were no services beyond the sites close to the parking lot.

We beached the canoe and began to set up camp. I could see that the CAPS folks would have a hard time getting all their gear to the search area. Brody and I could travel light once the tents were set up and our food and water stored. Red took to his little tent right away. We brought his favorite blanket from home so it would feel and smell familiar. The paranormal team wanted to get going right away, but I made them wait while we collected firewood and secured our camp.

When we were ready, we began the trek to where I'd found the naked mushroom taker hiding in the trees. Brody and I had to help lug some gear. I had a tripod in one hand and an equipment bag in the other. Brody had a smaller bag. The extra weight slowed everyone down and made the hike much more difficult than it needed to be, but eventually, we landed on the spot. I gave them a little background so they could decide where to set up.

"I found the guy here," I said, showing them the low hanging pine that mushroom boy had hidden under. "Up this hill, where it levels off, is the rock structure. He said they all made multiple trips back and forth from the river carrying rocks."

I led them up the hill to the rock wall where they deployed various Star Trek looking devices. Lights blinked, and beepers beeped as they examined the structure. It was a pile of rocks for crying out loud. What could it tell them? It wasn't alive. It was nothing more than a pile of rocks. They conferred and whispered like they'd found the Holy Grail.

"Up and down from here," I said. "To the river and back."

"Any idea what time this action took place?" one of them asked.

"Not really," I said. "Late at night, maybe even towards morning."

Red sniffed the rock wall, then cocked his leg and pissed on it. He was not impressed. He made no indication that it held any interest to him, other than to mark this new territory.

The ghost hunters frowned. I found it amusing.

"This is the place," I told them. "Knock yourselves out. We're going back to our tents to build a fire and get something to eat. We'll come back to check on you later."

They all looked at each other in silent communication. I believed that they wanted us to stay with them.

"We've done our job," I said. "We'll get you home too, but for now we're going to get comfortable. You're on your own."

The hike back was much easier without the added weight of ghost hunting paraphernalia. Red was having a great time tromping about the underbrush, sniffing and pawing to his heart's delight. This was doggie paradise. He settled down once I got the fire going, assuming his place at my feet. We still had a few hours before dark, but it was good to be prepared before it arrived. We ate a decent camp meal and provided our hound dog with water and Purina. All was well at remote camp Breeze.

"You want to go back later and see what they're doing?" Brody asked.

"I'm game," I said. "But remember we'll be moving in the dark. I've got a mark on the GPS so we can find them."

"You don't have much confidence in their techniques, do you?"

"None," I said. "Unless I see little white people with big eyes carrying rocks, I won't be convinced."

"Yet here we are," she said. "Facilitating those who believe in the supernatural."

"Why does it have to be supernatural?" I asked. "Either the Moonies exist, or they don't. No one said they were ghosts."

"The Moonies were something entirely different," she said. "Some kind of religious cult."

"You know what I mean."

"Moon-eyed People," she said.

"The naked freak didn't think they were ghosts," I said. "He thought they were real."

"Who put those rocks on top of that rise?"

"Who knows?" I said. "The rocks may have been there for centuries. Maybe the little people put them there hundreds of years ago. Doesn't mean they are still here."

"That particular formation isn't documented in any of the research that I've done," she said. "You would have thought that someone would have seen them before now."

"We've brought the experts to check into it," I said. "Let's see what they find."

"You won't believe them unless you see it with your own eyes."

"That's pretty much how I operate," I told her. "You know that."

"Allow for a little magic, mountain man," she said. "Let's rest up and then go watch what's going on."

I threw some more wood on the fire and stoked it up good and hot. I sent Red to his little tent and zipped him inside. He whined for a minute but soon settled down. Brody and I zipped ourselves into our tent and took an early evening nap. The woods were quiet but for the call of the katydids. The peace lasted for several hours until Brody poked me in the side and told me to get up.

"Let's go watch the ghost hunters," she said.

"Okay, hold on," I responded. "Lights, GPS, and some water. Wake up, Red. Going for a walk."

We had to get away from the dying fire to gain our night vision. We kept our flashlights pointed at the ground. Red seemed to know where we were going. He led the way but stayed close enough for us to see him. We ended up following him more than the GPS until we came upon the CAPS team. They were all huddled over various instruments, but no Moon-eyed People were in sight. It was after midnight; the moon was up and half-full. There was no wind. I was given a whispered command to come take a look.

Brody and I had done some research into the tools that this group was using in the field. I didn't understand how any of them would detect a ghost, but I was willing to play along. The first device I was introduced to was a thermal imaging camera from FLIR. That meant forward-looking infrared. It showed heat signatures in the dark or through walls and objects. It was currently displaying no anomalies. The second device was simply a digital audio recorder that was supposed to record electronic voice phenomenon. The idea that you could interpret static as voices from beyond the grave or from another dimension sounded like a hoax to me. The director of CAPS called herself a parapsychologist and assured me that it was standard practice in this type of endeavor. It wasn't alerting us to any paranormal activity either, but the recordings would be listened to and studied back at headquarters later.

They also had a full spectrum HD recorder and camera on separate tripods. Nothing was happening. Each member of the team was monitoring his or her device in silence. It wasn't much to look at.

"Four kooks in the woods at night," I whispered to Brody.

"Let them do their thing," she whispered back. "You never know."

We found a place to sit down and observe. In the silence, I was able to tune into our surroundings in my own way. I began to pick up subtle sounds like a slight rustling of the leaves above us. There was a light breeze that didn't penetrate the canopy over our heads.

We couldn't feel it down on the ground. There was a synthetic smell coming from the equipment and the cases it had been carried in. The director smelled of shampoo and girly soap; the men of deodorant and aftershave.

I heard the skittering movements of a squirrel in a tree. Red heard it too. His ears came to as much attention as a hound dog can muster.

"Stay," I whispered.

I wasn't deep into a Zen state, but I could feel the vibe of the woods around us. In my opinion, it was devoid of little white-skinned people hunting for rocks, or any other people for that matter. We gave it an hour before I signaled for the director. She left her machine and came to us.

"We're heading back to our camp," I told her. "We can lead you out of here at first light."

"We'll need some help with our gear," she said.

"No problem," I said. "Happy hunting."

I gave Red a pat and waved my hand in the direction we wanted to go. He faithfully led us back to our tent and was happy to do it. I poked at the remnants of our fire until some embers glowed. I added more wood and got a blaze going before we retreated to the tent. I produced a saved steak bone from my pack and tossed it into Red's pup tent. That would keep him busy until he fell asleep. If anyone approached us in the night, he'd hear them and alert us. All the hiking had worn me out, so I had no problem turning in.

I considered the CAPS folks and what they were trying to do. If I was of the same mind, what would I do? If I believed in their hocus-pocus, how would I catch the Moon-eyed People in the act? I mulled it over for a few minutes when it dawned on me. Mushroom boy had been hiding. He was well concealed and presumably as quiet as he could be. The little people didn't know he was there. The ghost hunters were right out in the open; spread out on the hill between the rock wall and the river. No little person worth his salt would show himself under those conditions. The researchers would need to hide and hide well. They would need to remain silent. They would have to hike in well before dark and get set up in advance. I decided to bring up my theory when we picked them up in the morning. It made as much sense as anything else about this mission.

Red whined and clawed at his tent before sunrise. It was enough to wake us up. He wasn't alarmed about anything, other than his bladder. The fire was out, but I took a leak on it just to be sure. Red chose a nearby tree. Brody went behind the tent. We had water and granola bars for breakfast, before breaking down our stuff and making it ready to carry out. We left our packs there and went after the CAPS team at first light. They looked like a miserable bunch when we arrived. None of them had slept, and they had failed to detect any signs of paranormal activity. They had already broken down the tripods and packed their gear.

I walked alongside the director on the way back. I explained my theory to her during the hike.

"I don't know that we'll want to invest the time in that type of approach," she said. "It's not what we normally do."

"You just walk into haunted houses and start monitoring your devices?"

"That's how we do it," she said. "With widely varying results. We want the spirit to know we are there, hoping they will contact us."

"Allow me to play along," I said. "The Moon-eyed People aren't spirits. They are living creatures, hiding underground during the day. Their ancestors were attacked and driven out by the Cherokee or the Creek. They've found this isolated place to continue their lives and their line. They ain't volunteering to make contact with you."

"Interesting hypothesis," she said. "You've given this some thought."

"We've been researching them," I said. "Reading what we can find. It's all myth and lore, of course."

"There is still room in this world for myth and lore," she said. "We try to use science in our investigations, but we have to allow for a little fantasy."

"If you don't believe you won't see?"

"Something like that," she said. "Most hard science is filled with skeptics. It's in their nature. Parapsychologists have to be open to the most fantastic of possibilities, or there is no point in the search."

"I have to admit that I'm a hardcore skeptic," I said. "No offense intended."

"But you took the time to think about this particular mission and explain a better way to succeed," she said. "Why do that if you don't think these people exist?"

"Giving you the most bang for the buck, I guess," I said. "I'm your guide. That's what I would do if I believed."

"That's very kind of you," she said. "But I think you may be conflicted."

"How so?"

"A part of you wants to believe," she said.

"A part of me wants to believe in Santa Claus," I said. "Doesn't make him real."

"Is that what you think we do?" she asked. "Wait by the chimney on Christmas Eve with our instruments?"

"I don't see much difference," I said.

"Instead you would hide away with a view of the tree," she said. "Not let Santa know you were there."

"If I believed."

"I can see I'm not winning any converts today," she said. "But thank you for your efforts."

"You're welcome," I said. "I'd be happy to assist in any future endeavors that might require my assistance."

We stopped off at our camp and gathered our packs, loading them into the canoe. The CAPS team filled their boats, and we all started paddling back to the parking lot. Red took his spot up front, which he seemed to enjoy. The ghost hunters were all out of gas by the time we landed. Brody and I carried most of their gear and loaded their vehicle. I shook hands with the director and accepted my payment.

"Better luck next time," I told her.

She didn't respond. She got in the big SUV and drove away. I guessed this would be our last mission together.

# TEN

We hadn't been called upon by any of the local police departments in a long time. No private jobs had presented themselves either. I was content to fish for trout and hike to waterfalls, but the lack of business was troubling. We toyed with the idea of taking a vacation; enjoying the warmth and sun together for a week or so, but my heart wasn't in it. My trip to the islands to assist Holly had scratched any itch I had coming from that direction. Brody didn't push it, so I let the thought go.

We hadn't heard from either of our two friends lately either. Angelina and Rominger were helpful when a mission was underway but absent from our lives otherwise. The isolation of cabin life was fine with me, but Brody would have liked to have more of a social life. She thought about getting a part-time job just to get out and meet people.

"I'm okay with that," I said. "But when we do get a job, your schedule will interfere."

"You can handle the investigations by yourself," she said. "You're completely capable."

"We're a team," I countered. "Plus we only have one car."

"Should we buy another one?"

"Inviting unnecessary complications," I said. "Two to maintain. Two insurance bills. More gas."

"You dropped almost ten grand on Holly," she said. "That would have bought you a decent truck."

"That's ten grand less in the kitty," I said. "Another reason not to spend unwisely."

"I didn't mean to imply that you spent unwisely," she said. "You did what you had to do to help a friend."

"Last time, I promise."

"I hear you," she said. "We'll see."

Spring stretched into summer before we finally got the call. Strangely enough, it involved the New River, State Park. Someone was terrorizing the campers at both the tent sites and the camper sites. A dozen reports of theft and vandalism had been reported in the last few weeks. The park gates were closed and locked every night. The campers couldn't leave, and no one could get in. There were no rangers on premises once those gates were shut. The campers were on their own until morning. We were being asked by the Ashe Country Sheriff's Office if we were interested in helping. I asked if we could sit down with them and the park authorities to discuss possible plans of attack, without committing to taking the job. The park itself was over seven-hundred and fifty acres. There were four separate access roads, all with gates. The camper area was far removed from the tent area. The canoe access sites were even further away and not easy to get to. I didn't immediately have any good ideas on how to approach the situation.

The first thing we did was print out a map from the park's website. It lacked detail but gave us a general idea of where things were and how far apart they were. You could drive around inside the gates at night from one end to the other; you just couldn't leave. Brody and I ran through a few different scenarios before we met with the cops and the rangers. If we split up, we could be at two different places at once. We could use our two-way radios to communicate, as there was no cell service anywhere in the park. That meant we'd each be alone during our surveillance. No reports had come from the campsites that could only be accessed by canoe. They'd come from the walk-in tent area and the camper area. There were two sites to cover, with two people to do it. All of the incidents had happened at night, which meant we'd have to stay awake and sleep during the daytime. This would be manageable for a few days, but if nothing broke in the case, we'd be looking for some serious sleep. We'd get tired and less attentive.

The incidents had happened every two or three days. If that continued, we'd have a shot at catching the perpetrators quickly. There was always the chance that we'd miss them. It was a big park. The camping areas weren't small, either. I knew that we couldn't remain vigilant all night long. We had our doubts about accepting the mission, but we hadn't had any other offers in too long. We decided to take the job.

We met at the park visitor's center two days later. The head ranger had his map prepared to show which sites had been hit by vandals and thieves. The Sheriff said he was attempting to get a volunteer from among his deputies to stay overnight in the park. He would be in plain clothes with no patrol car, but we'd have someone nearby with arresting authority. The Sheriff's name was Pete Powell. He was fairly young to be in his position. He was fit, athletically built, and clean cut like a soldier.

"Have you gotten a reference for me from some other department?" I asked him.

"I called Highway Patrol about these incidents," he said. "They suggested I call you."

"Have you learned enough about me to form an opinion as to my usefulness, or trustworthiness?"

"I initially had some reservations," he admitted. "But you were spoken highly of."

"My partner Brody is former FBI," I said. "My experience is much more unorthodox."

"That's what I was told," he said. "But your demonstrated skills seem fit for this situation."

"Let's think about a plan," I said. "If I'm down in the tent camping area and Brody is up here with the campers, where's the cop going to be?"

"Here in the visitor's center," he said. "Closer to the campers. I suggest having Brody with them. You'll be down below at a tent site."

"We'll need police radios," I said. "We have our two-ways, but they're on a different frequency."

"We got portables to spare," he said. "But you'll need to find a way to recharge them each day."

"Any of these incidents happen in daylight?"

"All at night," he said. "Well after everyone is asleep. Stolen coolers and propane tanks. Trash scattered about. Towels and clothing pulled off lines and thrown in the dirt."

"Anyone been physically threatened?"

"Not yet," he said. "But that's what we're worried about. Someone is going to catch this guy in the act, and a confrontation will ensue."

"Can the campers carry weapons?"

"With the proper permits, yes," he said. "Some want safety from bears, so we allow it."

"So a gun-toting camper might decide to take a potshot at someone stealing his beer," I said. "Maybe the perp shoots back."

"It would be a nightmare for the park," he said. "It depends on fees from campers."

"Are ATVs allowed?"

"Only on designated trails and with a permit," he said. "It's all shut down before dark."

"So, no campers have them?"

"Not even a golf cart," he said. "Other than the RV hookups, it's a pristine area."

"We've been out here twice," I said. "Down beyond the canoe launch in the wilderness area."

"Rough camping?"

"Yes, but only for a couple of nights," I said. "There's a lot more of the park that we haven't seen."

"There are parts I haven't seen," the ranger said. "Our intruder could easily hide out in the boonies."

"If he shows himself and we don't nab him, I can likely track him," I said. "I just need a starting point and some clues."

"How soon can you start?" he asked.

"Give us a day to take on supplies," I said. "Day after tomorrow."

"Check in here just like a camper would," he said. "Then, blend in."

"Is there an empty RV we could use as a home base?" I asked. "I can tent it, but Brody will need a place to sleep."

"I'll give a list to the Sheriff," he said. "Someone will volunteer, I'm sure."

"I'll need that day to make some calls," the Sheriff said. "Still need one of my men to step up for this duty too."

"We'll be here in two days," I said. "No cop cars."

"I'll reserve a tent site for you," the Ranger said. "Close to the restrooms on the riverside."

"Great," I said. "See you soon."

We took a quick tour via the surface roads before leaving the park; getting a feel for the full layout. There were several RVs on pads with hookups in the upper area. Half a dozen tents were spread out over the lower area, spaced well apart. There was a conference center midway down the hill, but it was currently unoccupied. Other parking areas and overlooks were vacant as well. It was a quiet place; secluded and wild except for the blacktop roads. The New River flowed through the grounds with considerable force, singing its song as it rippled over the rocks.

We had a lot of work ahead of us to get prepared, so we didn't loiter long. We drove back to the cabin to round up what we had and figure out what else we would need. I made arrangements for Red to stay at the doggie spa for up to a week. It would be unfair to him to keep him on a leash for that long, as the park rules required. I certainly hoped that we'd have our man in less than a week. If not, the Sheriff's Department wouldn't want to see the bill for our time and service.

Brody made a quick check of our handguns, stowing mine in my pack and hers in her purse. We put food in a cooler and water in jugs. The water at the campsites was supposed to be potable, but we brought a filtering device along just in case. One of us could always drive out during the day for additional supplies if needed, so we didn't try to take enough food for a week. After dropping Red off in town, we loaded the car with our tent, sleeping bags, the cooler, and a few smaller bags of goodies. We were ready.

We went to the Banner Elk Café for pizza and beers instead of cooking. It had been a long enough day as it was. The lodge section of the restaurant wasn't crowded, so we sat and lingered over one more beer.

"What kind of character do you think we'll be dealing with?" Brody asked.

"Could be another hermit situation," I speculated. "Except this one is meaner than the last one."

"Because he steals valuables?" she asked.

"And tears up stuff for no good reason," I answered. "He's got anger issues."

"Maybe he has a beef with the campers, or the park itself."

"We should ask the ranger about disgruntled ex-employees," I said.

"Good idea," she said. "Should have thought of that when we were there."

"Someone like that might know a way in at night even when the gates are locked."

"Or kept a key," she said. "Or had a copy made before they got fired."

"If such a person exists, that would be our most likely suspect."

"If not?" she asked.

"Some homeless person with a bad attitude," I said. "He figured out a way to get food and supplies, at least when the campers are here. I can't imagine he'd be out here during the winter months."

"The incidents just started happening recently," she said. "The weather has been pretty nice."

"Let's hope it's not a former soldier," I said. "I don't want to go against someone with skills."

"That would be the type to live out there in the wild, though," she said. "Not a drug addict or alcoholic."

"We won't know until we catch him," I said. "Or get a good look at him anyway."

"How're the knees?" she asked. "Are you ready to chase after our camp terrorist?"

"As good as they've been in a while," I said. "Though I'd rather not go running through the mountains."

"A gun will stop most people without being fired," she said. "Unless they are armed too."

"Let's hope it doesn't come to that," I said. "How about you? You ready to give chase if he runs through your area?"

"I'm good," she said. "He won't know what hit him."

We felt like we were prepared. We got a good night's sleep, thinking it might be our last for a while. I was good at napping during the day, but Brody wasn't. She worked best well rested, on her normal rhythm. I'd have to make sure she got sufficient sleep, even if it meant sacrificing some of my rest.

We fixed a big breakfast the next morning and took long hot showers. We locked up the cabin and headed back to the New River State Park. It was the fourth time we'd made this drive. Maybe we'd accidentally stumble across the Moon-eyed People this trip. Maybe our intruder was one of them; a fast running little white person with an affinity for camping supplies. That would explain why he only worked at night.

We parked in the visitor's lot and went in to see the ranger. The Sheriff wasn't there yet. We soon learned that he wasn't coming.

"He couldn't get one of his men to volunteer," the ranger said. "I gave him a key to the gate on 221."

"It will take them too long to respond," I said. "What am I supposed to do? Tie the guy up and wait thirty minutes?"

"His exact words were *tell them not to shoot anybody and good luck*," he said.

"That's a fine how-do-you-do," I responded. "We're investigators, but we're still civilians."

"Technically, I'm an officer of the law," he said. "But mostly I pick up trash and rent campsites."

"Can we arrange for you or one of your men to stay overnight?"

"If I had known in advance I could have tried," he said. "But we're on a strict no overtime mandate."

"Do you have any handcuffs?" Brody asked. "That would make it easier to hold someone."

"I do not," he said.

"Give the Sheriff a call," I said. "We're supposed to get police radios too. This is not getting off to a good start."

"You can always go back home," he said. "I would, under the circumstances."

"That's not how we operate," I told him. "We agreed to a job. We'll see it through if there's any way possible."

"That's on you," he said. "I'm locking up and going home when the time comes."

"Does Brody have an RV?"

"Yes, that much we accomplished," he said. "Follow me, and I'll show it to you."

The RV sites were very close to the visitor's center. They were quite civilized, with power, water, and waste hookups. It wasn't real camping, in my opinion, but it would be nice to have a central base to work from. The vacant camper we were shown was a small one, but it had a little fridge and a two-burner cooktop. It would do. The ranger went back to his desk, and we unloaded our food and some of our supplies.

We were on our own. It made no sense for us to follow through with the mission, but that's what we intended to do. We'd been through worse. Once we got Brody settled, we drove down to the lower parking lot. She helped me carry my stuff into the walk-in campground. I had the first site on the river, directly across from the bathrooms and showers. There'd be a lot of foot traffic, but that would give me a good view of everyone who came and went. We had our two-way radios to stay in touch with each other. We'd both sit and observe during the day, between naps. We'd stay awake at night hoping to intercept whoever was stalking the grounds.

I had a cooler, my weapon, and my wits. Brody took the car back to the RV and left me alone. I set up the tent and made myself at home, trying to blend in with the other campers already there. The river hummed a nice tune as it ran by the campground. It made me feel at home. I took a walk through the neighborhood, saying hi to passersby. Then I took a nap. The river sang me to sleep in no time at all. When I woke, it was late afternoon. I took a look around and saw that nothing had changed. No new campers had arrived, and everyone was settled in for the evening. I checked on Brody via radio. All was well with the glamor campers. There was nothing left to do but wait.

I thought I might make a fire, but the grounds were picked clean of fallen wood for the most part. The Rangers sold bundles of firewood, but they were a long way from the tent sites, and Brody had the car. I could have asked her to get some and drive it down to me, but I figured that I'd have better night vision without a fire burning. As soon as it got dark, all the other tent campers got a fire going in the pits that were provided. I sat alone in the dark, overhearing their conversations. None of them involved a nighttime campground raider. I supposed the Rangers didn't want the word getting out.

I thought about trying to bait the person into my site by leaving something worth stealing in plain view, but I didn't have much other than the cooler. I looked around for some other place to hide where I could see my tent but be concealed. The woods had been thinned out to create the campground. The only structure that offered concealment was the bathhouse. The other campers wouldn't appreciate a strange man hanging out by the bathrooms all night. I waited until it got even darker, scanning the trees for a good spot. There wasn't one, but I pulled my cooler out into plain sight and picked a random tree to hide behind. It would do no good if my target arrived from the parking lot. I was only protected from an approach from deeper in the campground.

I settled in and waited, trying to get comfortable. Hours passed, and nothing happened. My legs were getting so stiff I had no choice but to get up and walk around. I stayed quiet, using the trees for cover, but stretching my legs enough to resume the watch. All the fires were out, and most of the campers were inside their tents, if not asleep. There was nothing else to do out there; not even play on your phone. That was something that didn't bother me, of course, but I knew that most people who camped here were disappointed to discover they had no signal.

The night dragged on. I took up a station inside my tent, with the flap open so I could see out. I couldn't see the other tents, but I could hear anyone who came within the boundaries of the campground. No one did. As the sun came up, I lay down and went to sleep. Brody buzzed me on the radio just before noon. She was on her way to pick me up. Nothing had happened near the RVs either.

We fixed sandwiches back at her place, yawning the entire time.

"Did you get any sleep at all?" I asked.

"Not long after I laid down the other campers started making noise," she said. "How about you?"

"Same thing," I said. "I'm right in front of the restrooms and showers. I was dozing, but I could hear them coming and going."

"We should try to get more rest before dark," she said.

"I want to walk around down there and get a better feel for things," I said. "I can nap this afternoon."

"Not much to see up here," she said. "I'll come down and walk with you."

We had a nice little hike on the trail running along the river. I took note of who was where on the way by the other tents, double checking on the return trip. The day was bright and sunny with calm winds. There was no feeling of tension in the air. Everyone was relaxed and carefree; basking in nature. There was no road noise down here at all. The noise of the river dominated the sounds of the woods, but it was pleasant and reassuring.

We drove back up to the RV and cooked burgers for an early dinner. After Brody dropped me off again, I fell hard asleep in the tent. I didn't wake up until well after dark. The sound of someone running brought me to life in a hurry. I caught a glimpse of a shadowy figure as it disappeared behind the bathhouse. It was a man carrying something that I couldn't make out. By the time I got my shoes on, I knew that following him was hopeless. I had failed miserably at my assigned duty.

I called Brody to report my defeat. I was embarrassed, but she pretended that it was okay.

"Could have happened to anyone," she said. "Don't beat yourself up."

"I doubt he'll strike again tonight," I said. "But I'm awake now."

"If I drive down to get you he'll know people are about," she said. "He certainly wouldn't try anything knowing that."

"Our neighbors will be safe," I said. "Come get me."

I spent the night in the RV area with her, talking softly over a late night campfire.

"Maybe we should rethink our plan," she said. "We can't be expected to stay awake all night every night."

"Harder than I thought," I admitted. "This was child's play when I was younger."

"We should stay together and take shifts," she said.

"That will leave half the place unguarded," I said.

"It's unguarded if we're sleeping when something happens anyway," she said.

"Maybe we should bag the whole mission," I suggested. "We've got no cop on site. The ranger doesn't want to help much. This is looking impossible."

"It's only been two nights," she said. "So, we had a little setback."

"I'm going to speak with the Sheriff in the morning," I said. "Explain the facts on the ground."

"If you're good for a few hours, I'm going to catch forty winks."

"Go ahead," I said. "I'm awake now."

I stood watch while Brody got some sleep. Nothing stirred for the rest of that night, not that I expected any action. As soon as the rangers arrived in the morning, we were there to discuss matters.

"We need a cop or a ranger here to assist us," I said. "He could at least make sure we're awake and on duty."

"Talk to the Sheriff," he said. "This was their idea, to begin with."

"You must have called him to report the problem," I said.

"I was just doing what I had to do," he said. "I didn't hire you."

"Park rangers don't protect and serve?"

"Not after hours," he said. "I don't get paid for that kind of duty."

I used the office landline to call the Sheriff. I suggested that either he post a man in the park at night, or I would assume police authority to detain and arrest the suspect once I caught him. I hinted that I would use whatever extreme measures were necessary. I could see him frowning on the other end of the line.

"Now Mr. Breeze," he began. "I was warned about this type of behavior from you."

"Don't Mr. Breeze me," I said. "I was told there would be a cop here, that we would have police radios, and that I would be given handcuffs. Three strikes and you're out, Sheriff."

"Maybe you should just call it quits," he said. "Before you get yourself in trouble."

"Maybe you should cooperate before the taxpayers find out you're not willing to do your job when it gets inconvenient."

"You ruined that police chief in Banner Elk, didn't you?"

"Only because he needed to be ruined," I said.

He was silent for a minute. I could hear him breathing; stewing it over.

"I'll send a man tonight with cuffs and radios," he said. "He won't be happy about it."

"Thank you," I said. "Hopefully, we can end this thing quickly."

# ELEVEN

Deputy Roger Palmer arrived just before the gates were locked for the night. He came in a four-wheel-drive pickup, complete with a gun rack in the back window. He wore good canvas bush pants and expensive hiking boots. He was openly carrying his pistol on his right side. He looked formidable. There was a cooler in the bed of the truck and a rifle in the rack.

"We appreciate you coming out here," I said. "We know it must be an inconvenience for you."

"I would have volunteered sooner," he said. "But I didn't know about it until today. Sheriff said go, so here I am."

"Do you know your way around this place?"

"I've been here a few times," he said. "I'm pretty good in the woods. I can help with this detail."

"Excellent," I said. "Welcome aboard."

"How did you two get enlisted in this duty?" he asked.

"We've had some similar experience in neighboring counties," I explained. "I'm a tracker. Brody is former FBI. We've been around a bit."

"A tracker, eh?" he said. "Lost art these days. You got a dog?"

"I do but he's not with us," I said.

"So what's the plan?"

"We tried splitting up," I said. "We've got an RV up here. Brody took it, and I fell asleep on the second night, allowing someone to run through and grab what he could."

"Do you know what he got?"

"A bag of something," I said. "Food, maybe."

"Did you get a look at him?"

"Not a good one," I said. "But he headed uphill from the bathhouse down below."

"He was running, and he went uphill," he said. "Must be physically fit."

"We're open to any ideas you may have."

"Let's go down there and talk to the campers," he said. "See who is missing something."

"Should we try to enlist more eyes down there?"

"Can't hurt," he said. "If you want, I can stay down there alone tonight. I'm fresh. You got a tent set up?"

"First site on the riverside," I told him. "Right across from the bathhouse."

"Let me get you two some radios," he said. "I was told to bring cuffs too, if you want them."

"Both would be great," I said. "We can take shifts up here tonight. Reassess things tomorrow."

He gave us quick instructions on the radios and gave us each a pair of handcuffs. We shook hands and wished each other a safe night before he drove off to the walk-in tent sites. I felt much better about things. An extra man was just what we needed, and he didn't seem to be pissed about being there. He carried himself with confidence like he was comfortable in these surroundings and not just a street cop. He looked and dressed like he had experience in the wilderness. I figured we could count on him to do his part.

"I think he's got a little cowboy in him," Brody said. "A little cocky, maybe."

"He'll be a real asset to us on this one," I said. "Seemed competent to me."

"Cuts our work in half," she said. "How do you want to work the shifts?"

"Three hours each," I said. "I'll be happy to take nine to midnight. You take watch until three, and I'll handle it until sunup. We can switch that up tomorrow night."

"If we don't catch him tonight," she said.

"He just hit us last night," I said. "I'm guessing he won't be back for a night or two."

"You never know."

"That's why we'll diligently keep watch," I said. "I can't be asleep again when he returns."

"What if he comes when I'm up alone?"

"Yell at me on your way after him," I said. "You'll be fine. I'll be right behind you."

"Sleeping with your shoes on?"

"Probably not a bad idea," I said.

We ate a light meal and sat around a fire until nine when Brody went to bed. I let the fire die on its own and stayed up until twelve. No one sprinted through grabbing stuff. I woke Brody with a kiss, which almost led to extracurricular activities.

"Go catch a bad guy," I said. "We can take this up another time."

"Spoil sport."

"Duty before personal gratification," I said. "I can't believe I just said that."

"Me either," she said. "You are getting old."

"I prefer to think of it as growing up."

"God, we can't let that happen," she said. "You'll lose your boyish charm."

"Get to work, missy," I said. "Wake me at three."

I had no trouble going to sleep. Midnight is about two hours past my bedtime these days. It seemed like minutes later when Brody came for me, even though three hours had passed.

"All quiet on the western front," she said. "Nothing."

"I'll take it until the sun rises," I said. "Then we can continue what we started earlier."

"Best idea you've had lately."

My second shift was just like the first. I sat in a lawn chair up against the RV, looking and listening. The shadowy man did not visit us that night. The radio Palmer had given us was quiet. I allowed myself to relax slightly when the first signs of light crept over the campground, but I stayed vigilant until it was full-on daytime. I snuck up on my sleeping beauty and gently nudged my way into bed with her. She didn't object, not even when I started taking her pants off. It felt like we were stealing a few moments of intimacy, which added a new element to our lovemaking. We were always alone and isolated in our cabin. Now we were literally surrounded by close neighbors with thin walls. We both appreciated the change of pace.

"Pretty damn nice for a man who's been up most of the night," she said.

"I'm going to lay right here and wallow in the afterglow if you don't mind."

"No, go ahead," she said. "I'll check in with Palmer and greet the new day."

"Thanks, babe."

"No," she said. "Thank you."

I got another solid two hours of sleep before I heard Palmer's truck pull up. I rolled out of bed, put my pants on, and went out to greet him. Brody had already been briefed. Nothing out of the ordinary happened for him either. One couple had reported that a bag of lunch meat and cheese had gone missing from their cooler the previous night. The thief had left the bread. They hadn't even noticed until lunch time. Palmer had explained what we were doing and asked everyone down there to keep their eyes open.

Brody invited him to join us for breakfast, but he declined. He had a favorite breakfast spot not too far away. We decided to follow him and let someone else cook for us for a change. He took us to Shatley Springs Restaurant, a southern family-style place with good coffee. I pigged out on biscuits and gravy. Brody and Palmer both got pancakes and eggs.

"So where are you from, originally?" Brody asked Palmer.

"North Texas, ma'am," he replied. "Damn near Oklahoma."

"What brought you here?"

"The job," he said. "It was the first opening I found after the academy. Nice country."

"Did you ride horses and rope bulls and shit?" I asked.

"Daddy had a pharmacy," he said. "That wasn't what I wanted to do with my life."

"How long have you been on the job?" Brody asked.

"Five years now," he said. "I do like it here. The mountains, waterfalls, a little hiking, and camping now and then. Trout fishing."

"Us, too," I said. "We'll have to swap favorite fishing holes when this is over."

"That's a negative," he said. "Secret spots remain just that in these parts."

"Gotcha," I said. "I'd expect nothing less."

"But you tried anyway," he said. "Guess I can't blame you for trying."

We were all quiet for a few minutes, intent on our meals. I was glad that Brody and I had our little get-together that morning. I realized that Palmer was a good looking dude. He was much younger than I, masculine and charming in a southern sort of way.

"You married?" I asked.

"Not yet," he said. "Working my way through Ashe County. I'm hoping to parlay this job into something better somewhere else."

"You don't want the Sheriff's job someday?"

"Not here," he said. "Podunk stuff is all we get. Occasional meth case. Petty theft. Domestic disputes are far too common."

"I don't see you in an urban setting," Brody said. "You're a country boy."

"I'll spread my wings when the time is right," he said. "Meanwhile, I'll do the best I can with what I have."

"What's your take on the man we're hoping to catch?" I asked.

"Recently homeless," he said. "Doesn't have the skills to survive on his own. Maybe kicking some habit. Still young. Probably just came out here recently, after the weather broke."

"Reasonable assessment," I said. "Is homelessness a big problem around here?"

"Funny thing is you don't see them in the winter," he said. "They always seem to find a place to be when it's freezing cold and snowing. Family mostly. When spring finally arrives, they get all big in the britches thinking they're Jeremiah Johnson or something. That's our guy, but now he's reduced to stealing bologna from campsites."

"So he'll disappear when it starts getting cold again?" I asked. "Go back home to mommy and daddy."

"He would," he said. "But we're going to catch him first. Try to get him whatever treatment he needs. Make the campground safe for law-abiding folks."

"I like your attitude," I said. "Glad you're here with us."

"We'll get him in the next day or so," he said. "Keep on your toes. One of us will nab him."

After breakfast, we all went back to the park to rest up for another night of diligence. I was feeling rested, so I offered to take the tent area by myself, but Palmer refused. Brody took our first shift, which was the more demanding one. I woke early to take over for her, feeling guilty about not doing more. It was almost two in the morning when I heard something. It was barely a sound at all, but I was tuned into the night sounds. I had my pistol and a flashlight, which wasn't on just yet. I crept towards the source of the noise. I should have alerted Brody first, but I was too focused on catching an intruder. I didn't stick with our agreed upon plan.

Our borrowed RV was near the middle of a row. The sound came from the end, nearest the woods. I moved with stealth from camper to camper until I could see the last one. A man was creeping in the shadows, looking for something to steal. I raised my weapon and flashlight simultaneously.

"Stop right there," I yelled. "You're in my sights. Don't move."

The man didn't hesitate. He took off sprinting towards the tree line. I holstered my gun and went after him. I didn't start at full speed. I let my creaky joints loosen up a bit before picking up the pace. I saw where he entered the woods and got to that spot fifteen seconds later. I couldn't see him, but I could hear him crashing through the brush at a dead run. I followed the noise, using my light to see where I was going. My knees were holding up okay, but the noise was getting further away. I wasn't keeping up with the camp raider. I didn't give up, though. I kept plodding along, occasionally stopping to listen. Eventually, I could no longer hear the man. He had either left me too far behind or stopped himself to hide. If it was the latter, I could easily walk into an ambush. I switched off the light and stood still, trying to reconnect. I waited for a full five minutes but heard no movement. I was deep in an unfamiliar forest with no backup; not the place to be in the middle of the night.

I called off the chase. I wasn't going to get myself killed over some cheese and lunchmeat. I picked my way slowly back towards the campground, feeling defeated. At least I didn't get lost. Some tracker I was. Brody was awake when I returned and none too happy that I'd run off without waking her.

"Sorry," I said. "But he got away again. I don't think he scored any prizes, though."

"The two of us could have boxed him in," she said. "We're supposed to be a team."

"Spur of the moment," I said. "I heard something and just went after it."

"We need some operational discipline," she said. "He'll keep slipping away."

"Now he knows someone is on to him," I said. "He's going to be more careful."

"I bet he hits the tents next," she said. "He'll want to stay away from the RVs for a while."

"Good bet," I said. "We should let Palmer know what's up."

Brody called him on the radio to fill him in. He sounded alert and ready. Brody took over our watch, and I went to bed. I was pleased that my legs had cooperated and stood up to my late night run through the woods. It was a positive sign that I wouldn't be a slave to arthritis for the rest of my life. I had added magnesium to my turmeric intake, and it seemed to be working. The exercise was enough to tire me, so sleep came easily.

I chased the camp raider in my dreams. I ran through the woods in the dark in a never-ending pursuit. Small branches whipped at my face and arms. Old stumps threatened to trip me. I hurdled over downed logs and swerved through the trees like a slalom skier, but couldn't catch up to the man. I ran until I could run no more. I was miles away and lost. My knees hurt. Then Brody woke me up. The sun was rising, and I was in bed instead of lost in the wilderness. Over coffee, I suggested we consider a new plan.

"This isn't going to work," I said. "He's fast, so all he has to do is run. We need to be in a position to head him off."

"Both on watch at the same time?"

"With one of us between him and the woods," I said. "Take him down before he gets into the trees."

"Or up the hill behind the bathhouse," she said. "We don't have enough soldiers to cover the entire battlefield."

"Let's discuss it with Palmer when we see him," I said.

"I'll let him know you're up," she said. "Invite him for breakfast."

Our deputy partner agreed to join us before getting some sleep. All had been quiet down in the tent camping area, but he'd been up all night two times in a row. He said he wouldn't be much good to us if he didn't get a good ration of rest before nightfall. I gave him the details of my encounter with the thief and offered to rethink our game plan.

"We'd have to get lucky picking which zone he's going to hit next," he said. "But we could all lie in wait in one spot or the other. Try to surround him."

"And none of us gets any sleep," I said.

"Two up and one resting," Brody said. "Take shorter shifts."

"Might work," Palmer said. "We can refine the schedule as we go."

"I'd bet money he'll show up down below next," I said. "He should be shy about hitting the RVs again. Or try to wait until the camper that came after him leaves the park."

"You say he didn't get away with any loot last night?" Palmer asked.

"He was empty-handed when he ran," I said.

"Then he's hungry," he said. "He could very well try the tents tonight."

"All three of us will be there waiting for him," Brody said.

# TWELVE

Brody and I got a good meal at the Shatley Springs Restaurant before we began our preparations for another night standing watch. We drove down to the tent camping area and found Palmer still asleep in my tent. We made a little noise to wake him instead of invading his privacy. I didn't know if he had pants on or not. He crawled out rubbing his eyes and yawning.

"That river is a great sleeping pill," he said. "I needed that."

"Shake off the cobwebs before it gets dark," I told him. "We all need to be sharp tonight."

"Says the man who slept through the intruder's first appearance."

"Wait until you're my age," I told him. "Life hasn't worn you down yet."

"What did you do for a living before you started investigating?" he asked.

"Maritime consultant," I said. "Spent a lot of time on boats in Florida and the Caribbean."

"What made you move to the mountains?"

"We needed to get away," I said. "We've got a secluded cabin where no one bothers us."

"Do you miss it?" he asked. "I mean the sun and the water and all that?"

"It was great, but I've moved on," I said. "Just came back from a trip to the Virgin Islands, as a matter of fact. Didn't make me long for the old days."

"Sure is a big change for a person to make," he said. "But I guess you had your reasons."

"He wanted to give his lady a more normal life," Brody said. "The boat life started to wear on us both."

"We survived our first winter in the High Country," I said. "So I guess we're going to be okay."

"It wasn't a bad one," he said. "Other than that one big snowfall. I've seen it a lot colder."

"You're not helping," Brody said. "It was plenty cold for us."

We walked the grounds before dark, looking for good vantage points to set up an ambush.

We decided that all three of us would be on duty until midnight. Whoever was most sleepy would take a two-hour break and then replace someone else. Palmer said he could stay up until four with no trouble. We'd begin to see the light again soon after six. Brody and I would be together during the last two hours of darkness. One of us would remain near the tent to survey the other sites, while the other would take up a position behind the bathhouse and within hearing distance. We had the radios, but we could yell at the man which would alert the person in hiding. If he tried to escape using some other route, we'd have to give chase, but at least there would be two of us. If we could remain in contact with him until the sun came up, he'd have no place to hide. We'd call Palmer to our position and the three of us would corral him.

As Mike Tyson famously said, "Everyone has a plan until they get punched in the mouth."

There'd been no sign of a trespasser when Palmer called it quits at four in the morning. I took his place behind the bathrooms, and

Brody was awake and alert near the tent. Less than ten minutes passed when she yelled out.

"Stop right there. We've got you surrounded."

I heard her call and readied myself for a physical confrontation. I hadn't fought anything tougher than an emaciated meth head in quite a while. I was not a bruiser, but I was resourceful. If I could blindside the guy, I would gain an immediate advantage.

"Sheriff's Deputy," I heard Palmer say. "Stay right where you are, and you won't get hurt."

"He's running," Brody yelled.

I heard his footsteps approaching the bathhouse. I crouched, ready to uncoil on the bastard. At the first sight of him, I exploded on him like a linebacker, driving my shoulder into his ribs. I tried to wrap my arms around him like a good tackler should, but took a knee to the side of my head instead. He was down, but I was momentarily stunned. I saw a flash of light before the pain hit me. It was enough for him to get to his feet. I shook off the blow and focused on my foe. My head was clear, and nothing was broken. I got a good look at him this time. He was slightly bigger than I, fit but not bulky; a bit on the lanky side. He was all knees and elbows and knew how to use them to good effect.

Palmer came running around the corner, which caused the man to make a dash up the hill for the cover of thicker woods. I followed the deputy, and Brody was right behind me. If only I could have restrained the man at least for a few seconds, we would have had him. I used that two seconds to regain my functions after having my bell rung. Palmer was an animal climbing that slope. I didn't even try to keep up with him. He fired his weapon in the air when he got to the top, hollering for the fleeing man to give himself up. The guy never broke stride. Palmer took off after him once again. He was leading us deeper and deeper into the dark wilderness, but this time, we had an armed cop with us. Ambushing all three of us would be impossible without a weapon. I hadn't seen a gun on the man.

I settled into a smooth rhythm to conserve my energy. I was running at a good pace, but keeping my heart rate under control and not fighting for breath. I could hear Brody jogging along just behind me. She was in better shape than I was, mainly because she didn't drink like a mountain fish. I started sweating out some of the stored whiskey from my veins, even though I hadn't had a drink in days. Palmer's pace slowed, and I caught up to him.

"You okay?" I asked.

"Running out of gas," he said. "The dude ain't quitting."

"You good, Brody?" I asked.

"Good," she said. "Keep going. He's got to tire out sometime."

"He only has to keep running until we tire out," I said.

"Can you see him?"

"Too dark, but I can hear him," I said.

"Stay together," Palmer said. "This is his turf. Strength in numbers."

We did stay together, jogging along at a more comfortable pace until we lost track of our marathon man. We finally came to a stop in a small clearing at the bottom of a steep hill. It was a good place to give up our pursuit. If we continued, we'd have to climb that rise. None of us wanted to do that. We sat and rested until the sun poked down through the pines.

We were miles from the campground with no water or food. None of us had gotten much sleep. We were exhausted from the chase and adrenaline expenditure, causing foul moods all around.

"Fuck this shit," Palmer said. "When we get back I'm going home. They're paying me my salary, but it's for eight hours a day, not twenty-four."

"This guy is not only fast, but he also has amazing endurance," I said.

"Freakish," he said. "We're not going to beat him in a race of any distance."

"Then we need a new approach," Brody said. "We can't let him win."

"I can," Palmer said. "There's probably some real crimes I can solve back in the world."

"We do seem to be putting a lot of effort into petty theft of food and drink," Brody said. "It's not really worth it."

I was outvoted two to one. I hated to give up on a mission. It went against everything I ever stood for, but they were probably right. The guy was trying to survive off the largesse of recreational campers. They weren't overly harmed by the loss of a little food. They could go home and get all the chow they wanted, or drive to Shatley Springs for a good home-cooked meal. We still had a long hike in front of us. The walk was made more difficult by our feelings of frustration. Three capable adults had been foiled by one sandwich snatcher. It didn't sit well with any of us.

Halfway back, I heard the sounds of a stream. We were thirsty, so we diverted to it. The water was cool and clear. Not one of us hesitated to drink freely from the mountain spring. It was just what we needed. Revitalized somewhat, the rest of the walk was less miserable. Palmer didn't hang around for five minutes. He gathered his things, walked out to his truck, and left the park. I wanted to go home, too, but I was too bushed to do it.

"You want to lie down for a while before we pack up?" I asked Brody.

"God, yes."

We slept for a few hours before activity around us made sleeping impossible. Neighboring campers had been awakened by all the noise we'd made and were naturally curious. Palmer had made them aware of our mission and the nature of the threat. We told them what we knew and that the guy was still on the loose.

"Don't leave anything out where he can grab it," I said. "Put your coolers inside the tent or back in your car. Leave nothing you don't want to lose out in the open at night."

They left, and we started taking down our tent and packing up to leave. We noticed most of the others doing the same. There wouldn't be anyone left to steal from until a new group of campers arrived.

I drove out of the park with a bad taste in my mouth. Some slack-jawed loser had managed to avoid us in spite of our best efforts. It would be a negative for our fledgling business. Word would soon circulate that we had failed, even after insisting on police help and additional resources. Ashe County wouldn't be calling us again anytime soon. I could sense that Brody was fuming too. She hadn't had a chance to contribute. The men had let her down, and now we were going home with our tail between our legs. She had spirit. She didn't like losing any more than I did. It didn't matter that it was an inconsequential case. We'd been given an assignment, and we hadn't succeeded. It was a tough pill to swallow.

We didn't talk about it until we got home, which was after we picked up Red. He was beside himself when we showed up to get him. He spun around in circles and slobbered all over both of us. I hugged him tight and patted him down, calling him a good boy. He happily jumped in the car for the ride home. I stayed in the yard with him for thirty minutes once we got to the cabin. Brody went inside without unloading our gear.

After Red was satisfied with the amount of attention he'd received, I went in to find her. She was neck deep in a tub of bubbles, with a glass of wine at her side and some smooth music playing. When I stuck my head inside the bathroom door, I got the hand. She was in no mood to talk to me at that moment. I smelled lavender in the air as I retreated to the porch to listen to the song of the creek. Red watched the birds come and go from the feeders as I stroked his smooth fur.

Thirty minutes later, Brody came out with two beers. As she handed me one, I noticed she was wearing nothing under her robe. It was an enticing thing to see, but I was too tired to act on it. I really was getting old. After a few beers and several shots of whiskey, I changed my mind. I was not too tired, after all. Sweet sex with the lovely Brody took my mind off things even better than the booze did. Afterward, I slept for twelve hours straight. I woke up in bed alone to the smell of bacon cooking. The trip to the kitchen was an arduous one. The muscles in my legs were cranky, and my shins hurt like hell. On the plus side, my knees seemed to respond without much pain. I had given my legs one hell of a workout, and now I was paying for it, but any further damage to my joints seemed to be minimal.

"You look a little wobbly," Brody said.

"Everything is sore," I said. "But things held together. I'll be fine in a day or two."

"You surprised me out there," she said. "I didn't know you were a long distance runner."

"High school and for a while after," I said. "You know, a hundred years ago."

"You've still got it," she said. "But our fugitive runs like an Olympian."

"That gives me an idea."

"What does?" she asked.

"The guy's a runner," I said. "A real one, like in track and field. We should be able to figure out who he is. Get some insight into why he's out there."

"How do you want to start?"

"Go online and find articles about track meets and such up in Ashe County from three or four years ago," I said. "Failing that, we can call the schools. I can give a good description of the man now."

"At least it will give me something to do," she said. "I hate that we had to give up, even as insignificant as the case was."

"We'd need a small army of fast runners to catch him," I said. "Or a team of commandos."

"Which we can't muster to catch a guy who robs picnic baskets."

"We need a real job that we can sink our investigative teeth into," I said. "It's gotten real quiet now that the weather is nice."

"I'll call Angelina, and you call Rominger," she said. "Keep our names out there. Something will turn up."

We talked to our police friends who each told us that all was quiet in their respective districts. Most of the college kids were gone or would be leaving soon. Fairs and festivals kept the natives occupied. Prom night had even passed without major incident. The meth cookers were keeping a low profile in this part of the state, although there had been a big bust in Charlotte recently.

"Relax," Rominger said. "This is why people live here. Enjoy the calm."

Angelina had said much the same to Brody. A lack of trouble is a good thing for most people, but Brody and I were wired differently. I could enjoy serenity for a certain period of time, but sooner or later I'd get the itch for action. I appreciated nature, both on the boat and in the mountains, but I knew that trouble always lurked. That's how my life had been. I couldn't imagine things any other way. It seemed impossible that one could live for years with nothing but peace and quiet.

"Maybe we picked the wrong place to chase mischief," Brody said. "Soon we'll be reduced to spying on cheating wives."

"That's not beneath me," I said. "Does it pay much?"

"I have no idea," she said. "But I can look into it if you want."

"After you figure out who our runner is."

It took her several days of digging, but Brody hit on a likely suspect. There was a picture of Ed Pennington winning the cross-country conference championship from 2014. He was a dead ringer for the guy I'd seen in the park. The current version had a little more meat on his bones and a scruffy beard, but I was positive it was him. We found more photos from track meets where he'd won the 3000 meters events. The younger, skinnier Pennington had noticeably knobby knees and elbows. It had to be the same person.

Ashe County High School was in West Jefferson, just off Highway 221. The Huskies fielded competitive teams in cross-country and track and field. The cross-country coach was still around from 2014. I wanted to talk to him. Brody made some calls and arranged for us to meet a few days later for lunch. The coach chose Wendy's, which was close to the school. I hadn't eaten fast food in forever, but we agreed.

We arrived right on time and found the coach easily. He was wearing a Huskies windbreaker even though the temperature was close to eighty. He wore those old coaches' shorts like my gym teachers had worn so many years ago, along with a nice pair of New Balance running shoes. He got straight to the business at hand.

"Pennington was the best runner I've ever had," he said. "He was conference champ both his junior and senior years."

"But?" I asked.

"He was just an odd kid," he said. "Maybe he's a bit autistic, I don't know, but he was weird."

"Behavioral problems?" Brody asked. "Anger issues?"

"Not at first," he said. "But he was a real loner. No concept of team or camaraderie.

Zero social skills. All he wanted to do was run."

"It's not unusual for teenagers to be awkward," Brody said.

"Let me tell you a little story," he said. "We held a training camp in the off-season one year. I took all the kids to the New River State Park for twice a day drills. At night we'd sit around the fire and talk. I asked each of the boys how they became inspired to be runners. Most of them had a good reason; watching a marathon or the Iron Man. The Olympics was a common theme. All the stuff you'd expect, but when it was Pennington's turn, all he said was 'Forrest Gump'."

"That's it?" I asked. "Forrest Gump?"

"It got some giggles from the other boys," he said. "We all waited for him to expand on that thought, but it never came. He was done talking."

"What about his family?" Brody asked.

"Single mom," he said. "Just like Forrest. You know part of that movie was filmed on Grandfather Mountain?"

"Yes, we've been up there a few times," I said. "You said not at first. Did something happen later?"

"After he won the conference championship the first time, he was certain he would win States," he said. "Some kid from a private school beat him by eight seconds; not close. He lost his mind that day. Threw a tantrum like you wouldn't believe. His face was red, and his veins were bulging like he was about to turn into the Hulk. You would have had to see it to believe it."

"What happened after that?" Brody asked. "Was he disciplined?"

"His mother got control of him," he said. "We were done for the year, so I saw no sense in taking any official action. To be honest, he made the team contenders. We needed him for the next season."

"How did the next year go?" I asked.

"I've never seen any individual so driven," he said. "He won every race we had that year. Then he'd go out and run another ten miles. He was untouchable both running and personally. Never said two words all year."

"He won the conference again," I said.

"But didn't win States," he said. "Lost by a hair. Real photo finish. It was exciting to watch the two of them sprint to the finish. I was pulling for our boy even though he was a dick."

"How did he take this loss?" I asked.

"No, tantrum," he said. "Just defeat. It was his last chance, and he came close, but no cigar. He gave up life that day. He no longer had a purpose."

"No college prospects?" Brody asked.

"He was a poor student," Coach said. "Without my input, they would have flunked him out."

"What happened to him after graduation?" I asked.

"Stayed home with his mother," he said. "Failed at a few different menial jobs. That's about it. I certainly haven't heard from him."

"He's hiding out in the New River State Park," I said. "If that means anything to you."

"Hiding out?"

"Harassing campers," I said. "Stealing food."

"How do you know it's him?"

"I got a good look at him," I said. "Chased him twice, which didn't work out so well."

"I suspect not," Coach said.

"Hey, I'm young at heart, Coach," I said. "I didn't realize what I was up against."

"No offense," he said. "There's nobody around here that can outrun him."

"His mother still around?" Brody asked.

"As far as I know," he said. "She used to work at that bank right across the highway."

"Last name still Pennington?" I asked.

"Mary," he said. "Mary Pennington."

"Thanks for your time," I said.

"We appreciate it," Brody said. "You've been a big help."

"Try not to hurt the kid," Coach said. "I know he's an asshole, but I've got a spot in my heart for him."

"I've still got a lump on my head from our last encounter," I said. "But we don't want to hurt him."

I waited in the car while Brody entered the Lifestore Bank. She handed Mary Pennington one of our business cards.

"It's about your son."

"I'll call you later," Mary said.

We drove home and waited for the call. I popped a cold one at five o'clock and took Red out back for some Frisbee toss. Thirty minutes passed with no phone call. Red and I sat on the porch while Brody paced the cabin floor. I heard the ringing at six and went inside to listen to Brody's side of the conversation. She put Mrs. Pennington on speaker.

"Yes, ma'am," Brody said. "We're trying to bring him in."

"What's he done wrong?"

"He steals from campers," Brody said. "Mostly food, but folks are afraid of him."

"But you've seen him?" she asked. "He's okay?"

"He's fine," Brody said. "But he can't keep doing this. How can we get him to stop?"

"I never could get that boy to do anything," she said. "I doubt he's going to start listening to me now."

"You were close, though, right?"

"He was my life," she said. "He was a good boy too until that last day running."

"What happened Mrs. Pennington?"

"He was no good after that," she said. "Not good for anything. Lost all reason to live."

"He's still alive," Brody said. "But something is going to happen if he doesn't stop what he's doing."

"I want to believe that he's still got a soul," she said. "But he hasn't made it easy for me."

"Everyone has a soul, Mrs. Pennington."

"You don't know my boy," she said. "There's no light in his eyes. Hasn't been for five years."

"He loved you, didn't he?"

"Of course he did," she said. "I was all he ever had in this world. We were each other's only friend until he turned eighteen. That was right after that last race. He seemed to know that life was over for him right then and there. He didn't even try after that."

"Was he ever diagnosed with autism or anything similar?"

"I never asked," she said. "We're all God's creation."

"But he was different than the other kids."

"He didn't like people much," she said. "He hated school. Never had any friends other than me."

"Did you see joy in him when he was younger?"

"All the time," she said. "Here in our own protected world. But when he started running, I couldn't participate. That's when he started drifting away."

"It was something that he could do on his own," Brody said. "Something that gave him personal satisfaction."

"Except he became obsessed," she said. "I couldn't feed him enough to keep him healthy looking."

"Did you encourage his running?"

"I did," she said. "He was a thing to see in full stride. Like a gazelle, he was."

"Did he ever talk to you about losing that last race?"

"In his own way," she said. "It was like this; he felt special because he was the best at something. He didn't get his satisfaction just by running. He got it from winning. There was something in this world that he excelled at. He thought it was his birthright to win every race. Which he mostly did. In the end, he discovered that he could be beaten. It didn't mesh with what he envisioned for himself. He couldn't handle it. It made him question his very identity. What was he if he wasn't the best runner in North Carolina or even the whole damn country? In his mind, he was the greatest runner since Forrest Gump. When he found out different, it broke him down. There was nothing left to his fantasy. Life itself was over."

"Has he ever appeared, suicidal?"

"Not once," she said. "I'm not sure he thinks that's an option."

"What would make him come home?"

"I don't know," she said. "Maybe if I was dying. I'd like to think he'd come to see me."

"What about when winter hits?" Brody asked. "Will he come here? Will you let him stay?"

"I just can't say," she said. "He's always welcome here, but then the cops would find him wouldn't they?"

"He doesn't need to go to jail, Mrs. Pennington," Brody said. "He needs to be properly diagnosed and get the necessary treatment."

"Do you think you can help him?"

"We're willing to try, but he has to be willing too," Brody answered.

"It's not too late for him?"

"If he comes here, or if you hear from him, call us immediately," Brody said. "If we can sit down and talk to him before the cops take him in, maybe we can help."

"Why are you doing this?"

"I'll be honest," Brody said. "We were hired to bring him in. Now that we've talked to you and his coach, we want to do right by him. No one is ever a lost cause."

"God bless you."

# THIRTEEN

Neither one of us had a clue how we could ever bring Ed Pennington in, but Brody was interested in his described symptoms. She was much more empathetic than I was. I'd shown concern for those close to me over the years, and gone out of my way to help them, but I had little interest in the plight of strangers. My world had been much smaller than Brody's at the time. Now we shared an even smaller one it seemed. I had no choice but to go along with her wishes.

"Asperger Syndrome," she said one day.

"Ass, who?"

"Asperger," she said. "It's a type of autism. Trouble with social skills, tends to have an obsessive focus on one topic or performs the same behaviors over and over again. I think he channeled his energy into running. That was his obsession. From what we heard, he clearly lacked social skills. No sense of team. No friends. We were given all the clues."

"How does that help us catch him?"

"It helps us understand him," she said. "He was never diagnosed or treated in any way. Now he's an adult and doesn't know how to cope."

"What is the treatment?"

"Cognitive behavior therapy, social skills training, stuff like that," she said. "But it's usually done during early childhood."

"So no magic pill to reverse the condition?"

"Nope," she said. "It's a brain disorder. Not as serious as full-blown autism. Most become normal functioning members of society."

"What about violence?"

"Misplaced anger," she said. "Children throwing fits out of proportion to the perceived wrong, but no clinical connection between the disorder and violent behavior among adults."

"Makes me wonder how he reacts when the perceived wrong is real and serious," I said. "Like when we tried to trap him."

"He ran away," Brody said.

"I think he would have taken his anger out on me if Palmer hadn't shown up so fast," I said. "He didn't run for a few seconds. He was standing his ground after I tackled him."

"I'm guessing he can't make crucial decisions as fast as he can run," she said. "He was confused."

"That was it exactly," I said. "I didn't recognize the look. It's always fight or flight. I can detect when someone is ready to bring the fight. It's part of my defense mechanism. He was trying to figure out what to do next when Palmer arrived. That helped him make up his mind."

"So what do we do now?" she asked. "None of this brings us any closer to nabbing him."

"Go on about our business," I said. "No one is paying us to catch him now."

"No need to be heartless."

"It's called being pragmatic," I said. "A sensible and realistic reaction."

"I'm going to give it some more thought," she said.

"Me too," I said. "Thinking is free. I'll think on it all you want."

I think better with a beer in my hand, so that afternoon I sat on the porch drinking and thinking. Red was there with me keeping a close eye on the songbirds. Brody was working on getting the word out as to our availability to perform spousal surveillance. Sitting in the car with binoculars and long-range cameras seemed easier work than chasing a weirdo through the wilderness.

I told myself to sympathize with Ed Pennington. He was still just a kid. Big enough to hurt someone maybe, but not fully developed mentally. Capable and maybe even smart, just a tick off the normal scale. He possessed a superior talent. That's what he would always fall back on. That's what he was best at. He understood it fully and was comforted by it. I could never hope to beat him in a race, not even when I was young. So how could I deal with this problem? I decided some whiskey might improve the thinking process. I brought a bottle and a shot glass out on the porch. Red followed me to the kitchen then back outside. He'd been stuck to me like glue since we'd picked him up from the doggie spa. "You could catch him, couldn't you, boy?"

That was my first coherent thought on the subject. The whiskey worked, but I would need an article of clothing that had Pennington's scent on it. It would be best if it were something fairly fresh. I doubted his mother kept his clothes without washing them. I'd have Brody look into it. A little while later, another option popped into my head. I could track the son of a bitch down in broad daylight. Hunt him on his turf, likely while he was asleep. I could try to sneak up on him instead of chasing after him. If I missed him but found his camp, I could get something to present to Red.

I rolled that around in my brain for a few more minutes, picking holes in the idea. Red would pursue the man to the ends of the Earth, but they'd get far away from Brody and me. What would Pennington do when Red caught up to him? Would he try to hurt my dog? I wondered how people with Asperger's dealt with animals. I added that to Brody's list of things to do. I would sit there on the porch solving the world's problems while she dealt with the little details. The slight buzz I'd worked up gave me a smile. I was in a place in time that I'd never thought I'd find. I had my beer, whiskey, and a good dog. I had a fine home and an even finer woman. The creek was running cool and clear, feeding the flora that was now in full bloom. I gave up caring about what might happen to Ed Pennington for the time being.

Brody joined me and announced that we were now in the domestic spying business. We had a website and everything. All the local law enforcement agencies had been contacted. Cards and reminders would soon go out in the mail. Newspaper ads were purchased. All we had to do was sit back and wait for the jobs to come rolling in.

The phone rang almost immediately, but it wasn't a worried spouse. It was the head ranger at New River State Park. He sounded like he was in a bad mood.

"Our boy has run amok in the tent camping area," he said. "We've had to close it down."

"What happened?"

"He came running through last night with a machete," he said. "Sliced up every tent in the place."

"Was anyone hurt?"

"No injuries were reported," he said. "But they all got the shit scared out of them. Said he was screaming bloody murder and hacking away at everything around him. It all happened in a few minutes. He ran through and trashed the place and kept right on running."

"You closed the campground?"

"It's not safe," he said. "We're not taking any more RV reservations either. I'm going to have to post a guard in that area to protect what's already there."

"Damn, I'm sorry man."

"Nobody is blaming you," he said. "But I thought you should know. Thanks for trying."

"What are you going to do long term?"

"If there is nothing here for him, he'll have to move on," he said. "We'll reopen the camps eventually."

"Maybe," I said. "I've been thinking this situation through. If I think I can help, I'll let you know."

"We're not interested in hiring you again on any kind of official basis," he said. "We tried it once."

"I understand."

Pennington had acted out in response to our efforts to catch him. He was angry, but he didn't hurt anyone. It was clear that he hadn't considered that without the campers, there would be no food for him to steal. He had not fully considered the consequences of his actions. He was about to go hungry unless he found an alternative food supply or moved on to a different area. I didn't know if there were more campgrounds in the vicinity or unattended cabins that he might break into. That would have to be looked into. My list was getting longer despite my booze fueled efforts to solve the problem.

When Brody joined me, I hit her with a laundry list of questions in need of answers.

"Does Mrs. Pennington have something with her son's scent on it. How was he with animals and what other campgrounds are near the New River State Park?"

"What have you been doing out here?" she asked.

"Thinking."

"I see," she said.

"He trashed all the tents in the campground last night," I told her. "Sliced them up with a machete and terrorized everyone involved. They've shut it all down."

"That's not good."

"No, it's not," I said. "Now he can't get any food."

"You worried about him?"

"I'm trying to be more like you," I said. "I don't think his situation is entirely his fault. Thanks to you educating me."

"What do you want to do about it?"

"Still working on that," I said. "I don't want Red getting hurt, so ask his mom if he liked animals or if he was afraid of them. Sneak in the question about his scent somehow. Maybe I can track him, with or without the dog."

"What was the other thing?"

"If he's driven out of the park, where will he go?" I asked. "Other camps or cabins within a reasonable distance."

"What will you be doing while I work on all of this?"

"I was coming up with solutions to all the world's problems," I said. "I might go back to that, or maybe not."

"Maybe you could heat up the grill," she said. "I've got a London broil ready to go."

"Excellent," I said. "Sounds perfect."

I fired up the Weber, and soon it started smoking and smelling like meats cooked previously. Red took notice and woke from his slumber. He knew that sometimes treats magically appeared when the grill was smoking. I put the whiskey away for the night but grabbed another beer as I rescued the London broil from the fridge. Brody had it soaking in a teriyaki marinade. She was in the bedroom, presumably on the phone with Mrs. Pennington. She was good at conversation. I was good at grilling meat. Things were right with the universe.

Over dinner, we discussed her chat with the runner's mother. There was one item of interest in her home. She'd never washed his pillowcase precisely because it smelled like him. It was the only thing she could think of that would provide a proper scent. On the subject of animals, he not only liked them, but he had an uncanny way with them. Animals loved him, and he loved them back. He was a virtual animal whisperer, didn't matter what kind. Dogs, cats, horses, and even birds were putty in his hands.

"She went on and on about this," Brody said. "He was a regular Doctor Doolittle."

"Probably found animals easier to relate to than humans," I said. "That tells me he won't hurt Red. Plus she has something he can get a scent from."

"Are you considering searching a bazillion acres of wilderness for this kid?"

"You want me to let him go hungry?"

"I am not thrilled about you being out there for days on end with no help," she said. "It's not like you walk in and find him in a few hours. He's avoided detection this long for a reason."

"So we study the terrain," I said. "We've done this before. We know at least one route of travel. It's a starting place. I don't care how great of a runner he is, his camp ain't twenty miles away."

"Probably not," she said. "I'll print out some satellite shots from Google Earth. Maybe we can get a helicopter to make a pass or two. The Forest Service should be willing."

"Now we're talking," I said. "I'll go dust off the mountain man clothes."

"Good Lord," she said. "Let me have those. I've been reading about washing them in baking soda. Hunters do it. No scent at all. I'm not letting you put that stuff on the way it is."

There was no point in resisting. The clothes I wore to stalk the woods were beyond crusty. That was the point. They didn't smell like me; they smelled like dirt. They had never once been washed. I went to find them in the garage, and they were covered in cobwebs and a thick layer of dust. Brody wouldn't let me bring them in the house until I hosed them down and hung them on the bushes over-night. I had a pair of deerskin shoes and a floppy hat of undetermined material as well. I wouldn't let her wash them because I was afraid they'd fall apart. I hit them with the hose too and hung them up to dry. A good rainstorm the next day further rinsed them but made drying impossible. I left them hanging like any good hillbilly would.

In the following days, it rained and rained. My tracking clothes were still hanging in the backyard. Any residual scent left by Pennington in the park would be long washed away. There was no point in trying to hunt him now. I had no starting point to put Red on his trail. In the meantime, we got our first call from a jealous wife. Creekside Investigations was officially in a new line of business.

Mrs. Bronson suspected that her husband was cheating. He was working late hours and had developed a habit of taking a shower as soon as he returned home. This was unusual behavior for him she said. There were no other signs of marital strife; they still got along well and even had sex on a semi-regular basis. Still, she was worried. If we discovered that he was not cheating, that would be great. Could we follow him and find out what was going on? We accepted the job and made an appointment to visit with her the next day.

We drove to the Bronson home in Linville Ridge early the next afternoon. This couple had a few bucks. We learned that he was an investment advisor, working for an outfit called Edward Jones. His office was only a few miles away, on 105 between Banner Elk and Boone. She gave us a picture and described his car, a late-model Mercedes. Brody took care of the particulars of our agreement while I made a quick scan of the home's interior. Nick Bronson was a golfer, Rotarian, and all-around upstanding member of the community. His wife was attractive, although aging, and didn't work. He had a few extra pounds around the waistline but was attractive in his own right. They were the American dream couple, living life to the fullest in the High Country of western North Carolina. I processed as much information as I could before Brody and our new client were finished. I thought about the concept of infidelity, which I should have thought more about before getting into this line of work.

When I'd been married to Laura, I never once thought about cheating on her. I wasn't tempted. We said our vows before God, and I had no intention of ever breaking them. We were both committed to each other. After she died, it was a long time before I was ever with another woman. It still felt like cheating, even then. Brody and I weren't legally married, but we were still just as committed. I had been severely tempted by our now friend Angelina Will, but I found the strength to resist. I couldn't hurt the woman I truly loved. I just couldn't do it.

There was one time when I was dating a hot lawyer lady in Punta Gorda. She was way out of my league, but I was a convenient plaything for her. I guess you could have called her my girlfriend, but we had no serious commitment. I had rescued two Russian sex slaves and put them up in a cheap apartment in town. One day I went to check on them, and the prettier one of the two decided she needed to repay me for my kindness. She had no money. I put up a small argument but quickly gave into her advances. Technically, I cheated that day, but the lawyer turned out to be an evil witch so I never really regretted it.

I hoped that Mrs. Bronson was wrong about her husband. The only way to find out was to follow and surveil him, which we began doing the very next night. His work hours were nine to five. We parked across the street and watched him come out and get in his car at six. We followed him to the gym on Tynecastle Highway. We used the parking lot of a Mexican restaurant to keep an eye on his car. He came out ninety minutes later and drove towards his home. We followed until he arrived at the entrance to his gated community.

His routine was much the same the following night, except when he left the gym, he parked very close to us at the restaurant. After he went inside, we followed. He was sitting at the bar with a bottle of Corona in front of him. He was alone. We waited for some mystery woman to join him, but it didn't happen. He finished his one beer and drove home. We did not follow him into the neighborhood. His wife had given us the gate code, but we didn't want to risk him realizing he was being tailed.

The next day Brody called Mrs. Bronson. Her husband had arrived home shortly after we'd seen him go through the gate. He'd said nothing about attending a gym. Were we sure he was in there the entire time? Was he meeting a woman inside, or slipping out a back door? We agreed to find out if we could. That meant signing up for a gym membership ourselves. Fortunately, they offered a trial run of two weeks for cheap. Hell, I didn't even have anything resembling gym shoes. We had to drive to Boone to buy some for each of us. Brody said we could bill the Bronson's for them.

"Time and expenses," she said. "We can bill her for the two beers we had at the Mexican place too."

"Sweet," I said. "Maybe he'll stay longer next time. We can charge her for a meal."

The next time we followed him to the gym, we did a drive-by before coming back a few minutes later and parking a few spaces from his car. We signed in at the front desk and looked over the various apparatus. I had no idea where to start or how to behave in a gym. I'd always jogged, swam, and did a few push-ups to stay in shape.

"Try the stationary bike," Brody suggested. "It will be good for your knees."

We each mounted a machine that allowed us to keep an eye on Nick Bronson. He was alone and working out on a rowing device. He went at it pretty hard, huffing and sweating. He didn't seem to notice us, or at least he didn't recognize us from the restaurant.

I cycled for twenty minutes at a moderate pace. It loosened up my legs nicely, without the pounding of a run. I switched to free weights and did some bench presses. We moved from station to station putting in minimal effort. Sure I could be in better shape, but I was there to watch a man, not turn myself into Adonis. We left after an hour and returned to the Puerto Nuevo, the Mexican place across the street. As soon as we saw his car headed our way, we hurried inside and took seats at the bar. He nodded acknowledgement when he came in and took a seat further down the bar. He ordered his Corona. No woman came to meet him. We didn't follow him when he left, but Brody confirmed that he arrived home shortly thereafter. As far as I was concerned, the man was innocent. Our job was done.

The next day Brody called Mrs. Bronson to settle our business agreement. Somehow she got roped into a meeting with the local women's club in Linville Ridge. We met at the golf club a few days later. Several of Mrs. Bronson's friends wanted the same service. It would be nice to know that their husbands were as faithful as Nick Bronson. We warned them that they might not be happy with what we discovered, but they insisted. We left with six solid contacts and likely six easy assignments. We were husband watchers now; holding the fate of marriages in our hands. I almost wanted to sneak back to that golf club and warn all the men members that their wives didn't trust them.

Some of the Linville Ridge ladies had good reason to be suspicious. We stayed busy for the next two months trailing men around two counties as they carried out their elicit affairs. Half of those we followed were indeed guilty of infidelity. The other three were clean, as far as we could determine. Photographic evidence was presented where necessary. We became familiar daytime faces at the golf club. Enough retired men who hung around during the day saw us and figured out what was going on to end our campaign in that particular neighborhood. The ladies had friends who lived elsewhere though, and soon we were in high demand all over Avery and Watauga Counties.

It was easy duty, but I was always disappointed when we caught a cheater. I wanted some male clients so we could follow women while their husbands were at work. I believed that women were just as capable of cheating, and better at deception than men were. We'd made our name with the female side of the equation though, and it was a steady stream of business and income. It was also much less dangerous than any of the previous ventures I'd gotten into in the High Country. We'd managed to create a demand where one hadn't previously existed, which I found interesting. What else could we create that would drive business our way?

# FOURTEEN

Our connections within law enforcement sometimes came in handy. Angelina or Rominger could give us a call when a suspect left home or work. Police officers could sometimes get into places that we couldn't. They could also get answers that wouldn't be freely given to civilian strangers. For the most part, this was kept on the up and up, but occasionally the rules got slightly bent. Our cop friends trusted us, and we trusted them. It was a solid working relationship.

We had new business cards made which said *Marital Investigation/Discreet and Professional*. We soon had more work than we could handle as word spread to more and more communities. Each successful job led to several others. We were out on the streets six nights a week, reserving Sundays as a day of rest. Booze had been completely eliminated from my life as a result. It wasn't a conscious decision. That's just the way it worked out. I wasn't about to mix alcohol with business. I still downed my share of beer on Sunday evenings.

We'd forgotten all about Ed Pennington. It had been months since we'd even mentioned his name. That changed when we got a call from the Ashe Country Sheriff. There'd been no sign of our runner at the State Park, and the campgrounds had been reopened, but new reports had started coming in from two campgrounds to the north of the state park. I wasn't being asked to investigate. It was just a courtesy call.

A quick check on Google Maps revealed nine campgrounds within easy hiking distance of the park. A fifteen-minute drive by car wouldn't be hard to reach on foot for Pennington. The two places that he'd visited were River Camp USA and Twin Rivers Campground. They were both alongside the New River, just south of the Virginia state line, minutes apart. I wasn't sure what to do about it, though. Brody called Mrs. Pennington to let her know that her son was still alive, and still pilfering campgrounds.

We decided to drive up that way and take a look around. Both places were well kept, with clean bathrooms and nice facilities for both tents and RVs. The owner at Two Rivers was friendly and professional. She showed us around and offered to make us a reservation. It was a beautiful place, but we told her we had some more looking around to do. She made no mention of late night raids on her campers. The owner of River Camp USA was a bit odd. The place had some serious issues. The grounds and utilities were in serious disrepair. Jay was in no mood to talk with us about anything unless we were ready to rent space. He made no mention of Pennington's antics either. We left without making a reservation at either campground. I hadn't given enough thought to restarting the mission to bring the runner in. Chasing cheaters was so much easier. The jobs were lined up and waiting for our attention.

Next, we followed Wayne Camp from Banner Elk to a seedier section of Boone. He was an electrical engineer married to an older woman who stayed at home during the day. She said that he'd been acting strangely lately. That's all she had to tell us. He worked irregular hours all the time, so it wasn't coming home late that triggered her suspicions. We guessed that having husbands followed had become trendy amongst the women who could afford it, and Sandy Camp was keeping up with the latest Avery County "It" thing.

We followed her husband for two weeks. He went to a lot of different locations to consult on construction and rehabilitation projects. Some of these were in less than desirable neighborhoods. We lost track of him several times because there was no place to set up and watch him, but it appeared that he was doing his job rather than secretly meeting women. The man likes to get his drink on. We watched him down booze in a few different bars until it became impossible to follow him inside without him recognizing us. He never went home without hitting a bar, and he seemed to have no preference as to where he drank. He went wherever it was convenient in his travels.

One night he made an additional stop after his work and drinking were done. Between the Walmart and Highway 105 was one of those lower class areas dominated by trailers and section 8 housing. We could think of no legitimate reason for him to visit this place. Again, access to a decent vantage point was limited. We stuck out like a sore thumb. Brody dropped me off and continued driving. I had a camera, my weapon, and nothing else. I tried to act casual but soon ran out of excuses to be on that particular street after dark. Brody came back and picked me up. We drove to Walmart to figure out what to do next.

"If he's seeing a woman in this neighborhood he's scraping the bottom of the barrel," Brody said.

"Cheap whore or drugs," I said. "Maybe, both."

"Did you see where he went?"

"Nope," I said. "Could be any of a dozen places."

"Let's drive back by and see what we can see."

Wayne Camp was on his way back to his big ass SUV as we passed. We kept driving, with no idea where he'd come from or what had taken place. We had no hard evidence to convince his wife that he was cheating, but we had obvious suspicions. We kept them to ourselves — no point in alarming his wife for no reason. We kept up our surveillance, and the same thing happened several more times. We were never able to see where he went. We couldn't hang out conspicuously. We couldn't ask too many questions of passersby. We needed more information about who lived where, what went on, and the nature of his business.

Getting to the bottom of the mystery took more investigative time than any of our other jobs. Rominger hooked us up with the Boone Police Department for some background. We went to City Hall to go through property records. Brody searched for arrest records of any individual that we could identify as living there. We observed casual drug deals while casing the place when Camp wasn't present. Camp himself had never been arrested for any reason. He was an upstanding citizen who made a good living. There was simply no reason that we could think of for him to make periodic visits to a bad neighborhood. He never stayed long. He didn't seem like the type to buy crack in the hood. He didn't seem like he'd need fifteen minutes with a cheap whore twice a week either. What the hell was he doing there?

We'd been spending too much time and energy with this guy and getting zero results. I advised Brody to tell Mrs. Camp to come out and ask him what he was doing. A little communication can go a long way. If he denied his comings and goings, she could have a reason for suspicion, but we couldn't definitively say what he was up to. We had a backlog of other cases to get started on, but my curiosity was strong on this one.

I also didn't want to make a habit of not finishing what we started. Accepting defeat is a good way to make a habit of losing. We trailed new suspects at night but kept working the Camp case during the day. We got Rominger to visit the apartment complex in question and ask around. He talked to some officer on the Boone Police Department about the place. They started keeping a closer eye on it, spending some time on the ground, learning what they could. One of them caught Wayne Camp coming out of one the units at night and questioned him. That's how we got the real story.

Camp claimed that he was visiting a daughter that he never knew he had until recently. She'd learned about him through a relative's home DNA test and subsequent family tree research. Camp's affair with her mother was long before he'd ever met his wife. The girl was destitute, so he was paying for the apartment and trying to help her get on her feet, all without his wife's knowledge. All of this was relayed to us through Rominger, including the girl's address. We made a call on her and confirmed the details. Camp wasn't cheating on his wife or participating in any other unseemly deeds. He was a good guy after all, which was heartening. Finally, we could move on.

All of which made me revisit the Ed Pennington affair. That failure was still dangling out there, waiting to be resolved. I should have let it go. Our new venture was becoming lucrative and keeping us busy. There was no need for me to go tromping about in the woods of Ashe County in search of a man I couldn't possibly catch. He'd find his way home when it got cold, or get caught some other way before then. I couldn't worry about him too much. I had marital statuses to mend and rend.

Bill had been a member of the Elks for decades. He went to the lodge every Thursday night, except now he wasn't showing up at the meetings. He was diddling his mistress at the Best Western instead. Tom was spending some of his lunch hours at a trailer park outside of Boone. The young girl he was boinking was almost attractive, in a trailer trash kind of way. Jim was hooking up with his side chick behind a bar in Blowing Rock. They shared a few drinks after their automobile gymnastics were finished. Joe went right to the home of his second squeeze while her husband was supposed to be playing golf. The husband carried his clubs to the car and promptly drove to his girlfriend's house. We caught it all on camera, documenting times and places. None of them thought they'd ever be followed or watched.

We also tailed men who weren't cheating. One guy was driving to Tennessee to shoot his frustrations at paper targets at the gun range. Another would grab an hour or two of fly fishing once in a while on his way home from work. One stopped at a bud's house, where they'd drink a couple of beers while puttering with an old hotrod in the garage and bitching about their wives. We left the last part out of our report. A man needs to vent now and then. I suppose a woman does too.

We charged seventy-five dollars per hour, plus mileage and expenses. The mileage fees added up quickly. We also asked for a fifteen hundred dollar retainer to begin each case. It acted as a non-refundable deposit for services to be rendered. In the rare event that the final bill did not exceed, we kept the difference but offered the remainder towards a future case. We did not expect to be rehired by the same client once our work for them was finished. Therefore the minimum to hire us was fifteen hundred. Not once did any client balk at paying the fee. Those with guilty spouses felt justified in paying it, especially if the cheating husband was the breadwinner. Those whose husbands were found to be faithful were grateful that they'd been wrong about him. A few even held it over the heads of their girlfriends who weren't so fortunate.

Later in the summer, we finally got a call from a husband suspicious of his wife. He frequently traveled for his job. She was young and pretty. Once she had been downright joyous when he returned from a business trip, but now she didn't muster as much enthusiasm. He paid us the retainer and promised to alert us the next time he had to leave town.

We got his call a few weeks later. We'd already driven by his house, the wife's hairdresser, the country club and anywhere else he thought she might travel during his absence. He advised that the hairdresser was flamboyantly gay, so that wasn't a part of his worry. He doubted that she could get away with anything at the club without word getting out fast. We asked about credit or debit cards that we could track for questionable expenses. He said that she got a cash allowance each month, and all the household bills were taken care of by his accountant. So the young and pretty wife had paper money to use for her elicit purposes if there were any. We began shadowing the woman the day he left for Atlanta.

We spent two days following her to the grocery store, the yogurt place, and antique shops. On the third day, Monica drove her white Lexus into a residential neighborhood and parked it in the driveway of a modest home. We couldn't see whoever it was that greeted her at the door, but she was invited in quickly. She was in there for one hour. Just as she came out, another car pulled in and parked beside her. An equally attractive woman got out, and the two passed each other. If Monica's lover lived there, he had a second caller immediate following her appointment.

"That's odd," Brody said. "If they were screwing the guy, all sorts of fur would have been flying just then."

"It looked like they exchanged a polite greeting to me," I said.

"We need to find out who lives in that house."

"We've got to stay on her tail for now," I said. "Next time, we'll stay and watch the next woman come out."

Monica got her nails done that afternoon. She stopped at the market for some fruit and vegetables. She went home. We spent another week watching her run errands until it was time to visit the mystery man again. She showed up at the same time and left at the same time. The other woman we'd seen the prior week arrived a few minutes later and went inside. After she came out, a third woman appeared. She also spent an hour in the house. This dude had more stamina than I could imagine. I had to know who he was.

We used our connections and publicly available records to pin him down. His name was Vince, and he was a personal trainer. He was running his business out of his house, and as far as anyone could tell, it was perfectly legitimate. We'd let our imaginations and human tendency to expect the worst get the better of us. So far, Monica had done nothing wrong. I called her husband to report in and ask a few questions. Did his home have a security system and cameras? We couldn't watch the place around the clock so we wouldn't necessarily know if she took visitors. He said no one could come or go without him knowing, or finding out later. Did he want us to continue? If so, we'd need another retainer soon. He agreed to one more round but said he'd call it quits when the second retainer ran out. We continued to follow Monica as she went about the business of being a wealthy housewife.

We wasted a few more days before I felt compelled to call the husband.

"Are you sure you want us to keep going?" I asked. "We feel like we're wasting our time and your money."

"Did you ever have a gut feeling that you couldn't dismiss?" he asked.

"Sure," I said. "Is that the basis of your suspicion?"

"I feel like something is wrong," he said. "There's no evidence, just my gut talking to me."

"I can appreciate that," I said. "We'll step up our game. I'll let you know."

We took half a day to go back to all the places that Monica visited regularly. We checked them all for back exits or other access to the street that we couldn't see from out front. Both the nail and hair salon had back doors that led to employee parking, behind strip malls. The yogurt shop had no such exit. The last piece of the puzzle was the physical trainer's house. It had to have a back door, but where did it lead?

We drove around the block a few times until we located the backside of the trainer's home. It shared a backyard with a home on a different street. There was no fence between them, and the other house was vacant. A "for sale" sign was posted in the yard. We went back to tailing our suspect, and one of us watched her home throughout the night. Nothing happened there that we could see. When Monica made a move, we followed. When she entered a business, one of us kept an eye on the back door. When she went into Vince's house, we drove around the block and stationed ourselves within sight of the vacant home.

Monica walked out of the narrow side yard and was immediately picked up by a grey Ford SUV. We tailed it to another home nearby, where our subject and a tall, handsome man went inside. They emerged about forty minutes later. The man dropped her off at the vacant house. We quickly drove around the block again and watched her come out of the trainer's place and get into her car. The mystery had been solved. Miss Monica was stepping out while her husband was away; maybe even when he was home. She'd been good at covering her tracks, but we'd cracked the code.

I told you that women were more devious than men. She'd gone to great lengths to conceal her affair. The only person that knew was Vince, and he was probably being paid his normal fee to keep his mouth shut. We had Rominger run the tag on the Ford. It came back as belonging to Foster Jones. Monica's lover owned a chain of convenience stores and had some free time during the day.

I gave the bad news to our client, including the man's name and address. He took it stoically but promised to send us a bonus for our extra effort.

"Sorry, man," I said.

"No problem," he said. "You did what I asked you to do."

Somehow I felt worse for our first male client than I had for the women who'd been cheated on. I knew that was chauvinistic, but I couldn't help how I felt.

"Should I feel guilty for feeling his pain more than the women's?" I asked Brody.

"We're dealing with the upper crust of Banner Elk society," she said. "All the women are totally supported by their men. The man is successful and wealthy, and maybe he grabs a piece on the side now and then. The women don't work, enjoy all the luxuries they could ever want and are expected to turn a blind eye. In Monica's case, she was enjoying all the advantages of a wealthy husband, but she was the one who wasn't faithful. I can draw a distinction there. She was ungrateful."

"He is gone a lot," I said, backpedaling a little.

"No excuse," Brody said. "But cheating is cheating, whether it's the man or the woman or who pays the bills. They are supposed to be partners in life."

"Like us," I said.

"Exactly."

"Infidelity is probably older than prostitution," she said. "One of the uglier sides of human nature."

"Man evolves, but the inner animal can never be fully erased."

"The inner horn dog," she said. "Male or female."

I found the whole business depressing. I asked Brody if we could take a break from busting cheaters, even though the money was good. She told the next few callers that we were booked for the foreseeable future. We took some time off to go trout fishing, hike to waterfalls, and generally enjoy what life in the mountains had to offer. My legs were feeling much better. In fact, I was feeling healthier overall. Brody attributed this to abstaining from hard liquor and cutting back on the beer. I couldn't argue with her logic. I had regained a spring in my step and had an improved outlook on life.

I kept that positive attitude and even started working out a little. I'd drive down the mountain to Valle Crucis and walk the trails in the park at a brisk pace. I used the kid's swing set for pull-ups and did my pushups in the grass. When I was finished, I'd toss a line in the Watauga River. Eventually, I started running again, and my knees didn't complain. I was beating back Old Man Time, holding off the aging process for a later date.

We were enjoying the High Country again, but there was one little loose end that began to nag me anew. We'd taken an interest in Ed Pennington then gotten sidetracked. I brought it up over dinner with Brody.

"You realize that we made a complicated diagnosis of a man we've never met," I said. "We're not qualified to call it Asperger's or any other kind of autism. What if he's just a fucked up individual? An asshole?"

"His coach thought he was an asshole, but still had a soft heart about him," she said. "He must have some redeeming qualities."

"His mother loves him," I said. "But I suppose Charlie Manson's mom loved him too."

"Our guy isn't a killer," she said. "He's a food thief. He's surviving the only way he knows how. You made friends with the Beech Mountain Hermit. Not much difference."

"That guy depended on remaining invisible," I said. "Pennington depends on being able to outrun everyone. Plus he ruined all those tents in a hissy fit. There's an edge to him like he might hurt somebody."

"What do they say about cornered rats?"

"I can't help but think some camper is going to jump him eventually and he'll kick the crap out of them to avoid capture," I said. "He can't cope with other people. He's cast himself out of society, yet he depends on other people for food. It won't end well."

"What can we do?"

"I don't know yet," I admitted. "But it's bothering me. I'm going to give it some more thought."

"I'll call his mom."

I called the Ashe County Sheriff.

"What's going on at the campgrounds lately?" I asked.

"Looks like your boy has moved south," he said. "He's operating outside the park boundaries."

"South?"

"There's a whole string of campgrounds surrounding the Thurmond Chatham Wildlife Area," he said. "Minor reports spread out amongst them. Food missing, a knife stolen, shit like that."

"Thanks," I said. "At least we know he's still alive."

"What's your interest in this anyway?" the Sheriff asked.

"His mother asked us to look out for him if we could."

"She hired you?"

"Not exactly," I said. "If we do anything, it will be on our own dime."

"Highway Patrol is driving through there once a night," he said. "But that's not much of a help. We can't post guards at a half-dozen different campgrounds every night."

"I understand," I said. "Appreciate the info."

# FIFTEEN

Mrs. Pennington spoke to Brody's softer side, practically begging us to do something; anything, to get her son to come home. Brody couldn't offer her any guarantees. We didn't know that we could help at all, or even if we wanted to invest our energies into a solution. Ed was a tough one. I'd tracked people down, even in life-threatening situations, but none of them had the speed or stamina of this guy. I could track him all I wanted, but if I couldn't catch up to him, it wouldn't make much of a difference.

My only remaining option was to sneak up to him. If I could go full stealth and quietly move in, maybe I'd have a chance. My fear with that plan was the fight that might ensue. How could I prevent him from running away? All he needed was a moment of separation, and he'd be gone in a flash. Pouncing on him in his sleep was one thing. Restraining him was something else all together. Two of us might be able to lasso his feet, but that would mean Brody would have to move as quietly as I did. Her ability to move like smoke was not on the same level as mine. Asking her to crawl through the woods for many hours, maybe even days, seemed out of the question.

Another option was to use Red somehow. Red could certainly trail the man to the ends of the Earth, but what then? I'd have to keep up with him, or at least stay close enough to move in once he cornered his target. It all led to a physical showdown with an unpredictable opponent. I didn't want to hurt him, and I didn't want to get hurt myself. I didn't know how to talk to him or what to say once I confronted him. His potential disability made him different from the average man. There was no way to know how he would react.

I kept spinning all these different scenarios around in my head, searching for one that would end peacefully. The more I thought about it, the more I felt that I had to do something, but that led me no closer to a plan that gave me confidence. I'd gotten comfortable bouncing ideas off of Brody, so that's what I did. As usual, she got right to the heart of the situation.

"You've lost a step," she said. "You couldn't run down that Belmonti guy because your knees gave out on you. You're not twenty-something anymore. So now you're hesitant. You need to get that mountain man cockiness back. Use your wits and wisdom to overcome youth and inexperience."

"Beat him in the woods," I said. "Outsmart him somehow."

"That's your sweet spot these days," she said. "You've got to own that mountain like you've done before. Refuse to be beaten."

"That gives me an idea," I said. "Thanks for the inspiration."

"You want to share?"

"Not yet," I said. "I've got to get my head right. I'll need my mountain Zen clothes."

"Can I wash them like I wanted to?"

"All that rain should be sufficient," I said. "Nothing more natural than that."

"Hanging clothes on a bush in the rain is not the same as a good washing."

"After this," I said. "One more time, and then you can have at it."

"It's like a good luck charm for you, isn't it?"

"Makes me think of Pop and how he moved in the woods," I said. "He was a true ghost."

"Have you been up there to his cave lately?"

"It's been a while," I said. "We've been busy elsewhere."

"Maybe you should hike up there," she said. "Get back to your roots."

"Good idea," I said. "I think you understand more than you let on."

"Become one with the mountain," she said. "That will straighten you out."

"It will be a good practice run," I said. "You're so smart."

"I've got to earn my keep somehow," she said. "Because I'm not going out into the wilderness with you. That's your bag."

The clothes that I liked to wear to sneak about the woods were as crusty as week old bread, and maybe a little moldy too. I had to break down and let Brody wash them in baking soda. I wouldn't let her put them in the dryer, though. I hung them up outside so they could breathe in the fresh mountain air. I got out my lightest backpack and started choosing items for a trip up McGuire Mountain. Red was quite interested in what I was doing.

"Sorry, buddy," I said. "I'm going it alone this time."

I left early the next morning, climbing the hill out back and ducking into the trees. I shot Brody a wave before I disappeared. She was shaking her head as she waved back, probably thinking what a fool I was. I hiked at a crisp pace for most of the way, testing my legs. I felt strong. Before I got too close to the plateau where old Pop had once grown his weed, I slowed and stopped to rest. I sat on a flat rock and took in my surroundings. This trip had once been intimately familiar to me, but I hadn't been up here in a long time.

I relaxed and slowed my breathing, taking in the sights, sounds, and smells of my surroundings. The sound of the creek was ever present, but I also picked up the bird songs and the rustling of the leaves. I smelled pine most of all, but under it was earth and wood. I remained still, letting it all come to me;

feeling the vibrations of nature. Eventually, I began to drift through the trees as if someone was hunting me. No one was there, but I wanted to feel what it was like. I needed to get back into a certain mode; becoming a ghost-like Pop. Not even the birds could know I was there. I slid my deerskin shoes between the leaves and sticks without making a sound. I was never in the open, instead slipping from tree to rock in smooth motions that couldn't be heard. I forced myself to keep the progress slow and silent. Eventually, I came to a place where I could see out over the plateau. I watched it for ten minutes, making sure I was alone. Finally, I gave up my hiding spot and walked through the dirt of the old pot farm. I was king of the mountain, and it felt good.

I climbed up onto the rock ledge that led to Pop's cave. The brush blocking its entrance had browned and fallen off in places. I poked my head inside and found nothing disturbed. A few spider webs had grown in the corners, so I grabbed a stick and swept them away. I crawled into the corner where Pop slept and sat on the musty bedroll, looking back out of the entrance. He had lived here for years, unbeknownst to any of us below. This had been his mountain. He had staked his claim on a piece of no man's land and survived without stealing what he needed to live. He was likely the last of the true mountain men. I was only playing at it, but I would need the skills he taught me to handle Ed Pennington.

I sat in silent contemplation for a long time before boredom got the best of me. I decided to redo the branches that concealed the cave entrance. I don't know why it just seemed like something I ought to do. I used my heavy knife to chop new pine limbs and dragged them along the ledge. I kicked the dead and brown stuff over the side and went to work rearranging the new, green stuff. When I finished, I realized it was too late to make it back down the mountain before dark. I climbed off the ledge, gathered up the dead limbs, and took them away; hiding them in thick brush far from the cave. I gathered up some sticks and dried branches to make a fire. I built it on a flat spot there on the plateau and warmed myself as the sun went down.

I asked myself a question. Did I give a shit about Ed Pennington, or was it more important for me to win? I did feel sorry for his mother. I knew that Brody had genuine compassion, but I didn't seem to care as much about the near-anonymous man. Maybe if I knew him personally, I'd sympathize. I had honestly cared about some of my old friends down in Florida, so I had that capacity. I'd even put myself in danger to drag One-legged Beth away from the mangrove druggies. I'd rescued those Russian girls in Pelican Bay. I'd clubbed a much bigger man in the head with a hammer to prevent him from raping a young Cuban girl. I didn't have to do any of those things. I did them because I cared.

Since moving to the mountains, I'd had even less social interaction. I didn't have friends here. I had to fly all the way to the Caribbean to help someone that I was once close to, and I'd probably never see her again. So why bust my balls over this Pennington character? I needed a good reason to care about his plight, but all I could come up with was pleasing Brody, and maybe proving to myself that I still had what it takes.

I sat there by the fire and tried to put myself in his shoes. He was alone in the wilderness, just like I was at that point in time. Was he creeping into a campground to nab a quick meal? Was he asleep somewhere deep in the forest? What did he think about besides food and escape? We thought he might have some level of autism, but that didn't mean that he didn't have all sorts of thoughts running through his head. He just wasn't good at verbalizing them. His social skills were far more stunted than mine, but it wasn't his fault. I chose to be a recluse, even enjoyed it sometimes. He had chosen a similar path, in his own way. People sucked, so he avoided them. We had that much in common.

I turned my thoughts to bringing him in. Outrunning him was out of the question, even though I was as fit as I'd been in a long time. I could track him down, find his camp, and try to talk to him, but I didn't expect him to listen. I could have Red chase after him, but to what end? The answer stayed just out of reach. I wasn't able to devise a plan that I knew would work. I got tired of thinking about it. I'd have to resort to my old method of bringing missions to a successful conclusion. I would wing it.

Unburdened with heavy thoughts, I doused the fire with water from the creek and made my way in the dark back to the cave. It was peaceful up there but in a lonely sort of way. I didn't mind sleeping on an ancient bed of blankets and a sleeping bag, but it was much nicer to sleep next to Brody in a warm, comfortable bed. I toned down all those thoughts and closed my eyes. The creek sang me to sleep just like it did at the cabin.

Pennington ran in my dreams for most of the night. He kept looking for that finish line that never came. He had fear in his eyes, not of me, but of some unseen danger. He would look back over his shoulder without breaking stride. He ran all the way to the ocean, and when he got there, he turned around and ran all the way to another ocean. One day, he would have to stop. That's when I could get through to him.

It took me a minute to realize where I was when I woke up. It was still dark in the cave, but the sun was starting to show itself above the ridges to the east. I crawled out of my hole and pissed over the edge, creating a tiny waterfall that pooled in the dirt below. I drank some water and ate a granola bar for breakfast, hoisted my pack, and climbed down onto the plateau. A lot had gone down in that place, but no one ever came here anymore. It felt like sacred ground. Cody Banner had killed Pop here, and later I'd killed Banner near the same spot. Brody and I had harvested the weed crop and lugged it all down the mountain.

This is where I'd learned to walk like smoke. That meant something to me, as I'd need to use my mountain skills to perfection if I wanted a chance against Pennington. I stood there and soaked in the aura of the place before turning and starting the trek home. I felt like I was ready to take my game to Ashe County. I'd gotten what I needed from this place. I was as ready as I'd ever be.

Brody was out on the porch tending to her plants. We had flowers, bird seed for the songbirds, and hummingbird feeders out there. It was an oasis where we could sit and watch the creek go by, made homey by a woman's touch.

"How'd it go, mountain man?" she asked.

"It went well," I answered. "I'm ready to face Pennington."

"You came up with a plan?"

"Nope, just gonna wing it," I said.

"That sounds like the old Breeze," she said. "Now take Red out and wing a Frisbee or something. He's been up my butt since you left."

I played with my hound dog for a solid hour. He would run forever if I let him. I couldn't help but think there was some way he could help me on my mission, but I couldn't figure out exactly how. I was going alone, at least at first. If I found the need to enlist Red I would. I'd learn the lay of the land first, find Pennington's camp, and take it from there. Something would come my way; some opportunity that I would grasp. I was going into the unknown, but I would solve the riddle. I'd bring the man child home somehow.

That night I studied a map of the area I'd be searching. There were five campgrounds on the fringes of the Thurmond Chatham

Wildlife Area. There was a state park at Stone Mountain to the east. Raccoon Holler Campground was to the west, outside the boundaries of state land. Multiple creeks intersected the wildlife area. The Blue Ridge Parkway skirted the northern boundaries. Longbottom Road ran along the southern edge. There was a valley right in the center that was split by Lovelace Creek. The closest campground to Lovelace was Doughton Park. The other camping areas were along Meadow Fork. A man could get good and lost in between. That's where I figured Pennington was holed up.

I prepared for a long stay in the wilderness. I planned to set up camp myself, and use it as a base of operations. Once I located Pennington's camp, I could relocate at will, keeping him within striking distance. I put a fully charged cell phone in my pack but left it turned off. I'd only use it if I needed Brody to come pick me up. If I couldn't get a signal, I'd have to hike until I found one. I had a GPS, pistol, food and water, and a tent. I had a knife and even a fishing rod. I rolled a blanket and attached it to the bottom of my pack. I could take fish and water from the streams. If I got desperate, I could shoot small game with the gun. I had a Zippo lighter to start fires with, plus spare fluid and flints. I planned to wear my mountain Zen clothes the entire time, but I packed extra socks and underwear. It was a heavy load, but I wouldn't be carrying it while hunting my prey. I just needed to pack it all into the interior and set up camp.

I had Brody drop me off at the Flat Rock Ridge trailhead, off Longbottom Road. I warned her that I might be gone for a week or more. I was determined to see this through. I had all my gear, and there was no point in turning back now. She wished me luck and gave me an extended hug.

"Be safe, Breeze," she said. "I know you need to do this, but come home to me in one piece."

"I will," I said. "I promise."

The hike started smoothly as I made my way through Grassy Gap to the Basin Creek Trail. That's where I veered off the worn trail of previous hikers and set off into the wild. I walked north along Basin Creek, which was about halfway between the Doughton Park Recreation Area and Lovelace Creek. I found a good spot that overlooked the valley but was below the higher elevations of the wildlife area. The hike didn't bother me at all. I still felt strong. I used the remaining daylight to pitch my tent and set up for the long haul. I gathered rocks to form a fire ring and got a blaze going just as it started getting dark. I left what food I had in the pack, and put the pack inside the tent. That way, neither bears nor Pennington could steal it. I heated the meat from a military-style meal in a tin cup over the fire. It reminded me of my army days, but back then they called them C-rations, and they came in a cardboard box. They're MREs now, meals ready to eat. You can't stop progress.

# SIXTEEN

The tent and bedroll were a step up from the cave on top of McGuire Mountain. The air was fresh and clean, I had a good spot close to the creek, and I was as far from civilization as I could get in the wildlife area. Getting there and setting up had not worn me out. I was ready to begin tracking down Pennington. I slept well, with no dreams to haunt me. After breakfast and a morning constitutional, I set out to find my man. I used the GPS to keep track of where I was, meandering along the creek. I moved slowly and silently, stopping occasionally to listen. I worked a grid back and forth from the creek's edge, heading north. Half the day went by, and no sign of him was seen. I had to turn around and head back.

On the second day, I moved much faster until I got to the point where I'd left off. It took half the time to cover the ground. I started a new grid and searched until late in the afternoon. There was still no fugitive to be found. It was dark before I got back to camp. I ate and slept, and the next morning I packed my gear and hiked it all further into the woods. I remade camp near where I'd given up the previous day's search. It was much more difficult to travel with the extra weight. There would be no searching that day.

I found his camp on the third day, or at least someone's camp. The little army surplus pup tent was zipped up tight. He could be inside sleeping or not home at the moment. I sat down on a log and waited. Three hours later, Pennington crawled out of the tent.

"Good morning, Sleeping Beauty," I said, startling him.

"Who are you, and what are you doing here?"

"Your mother misses you," I said.

"How would you know?"

"I talk to her," I said. "She asked me to find you."

He was fully dressed, including beat up running shoes. I could tell he was about to run.

"Go ahead," I said. "I'll find you again. You can't escape me."

He eased away from the tent and jogged off into the woods. I let him go. There was no point in running after him. I'd found him once, and I'd find him again. I took a leisurely hike back to my camp and relaxed for the rest of the afternoon. Just before dark, I snuck back to the perimeter of Pennington's camp. I watched him pack up his few belongings and take down his tent. I did not reveal my presence. Instead, I followed him until he stopped and started setting up a new camp. I marked it on my GPS and snuck away. I returned the next day to pay him a second visit. He was making a sandwich outside the tent.

"They taste better when they're not stolen," I said.

He nearly jumped out of his skin at the sound of my voice.

"You again," he said. "Leave me alone."

"Don't run off yet," I said. "Go ahead and eat."

He took another bite, eyeing me suspiciously.

"You some kind of survivalist?" He asked. "Special Forces or something?"

"Nothing like that," I said. "I just like wandering around in the woods. Helps me clear my head."

"How did you find me so fast?"

"I followed you yesterday when you relocated," I said. "You're not so fast with a heavy pack on."

"I'll go so far; you'll never find me."

"But why?" I asked. "Nice warm bed for you at home. Mom's cooking too."

"Can't go back now," he said. "I'd be in too much trouble."

"Not so much we can't fix it," I said. "Come on back with me, and I'll help take care of things."

"I don't know you," he said. "I don't trust folks I don't know."

"Your coach was asking about you," I said. "He's worried about you too."

"That was a long time ago," he said. "Don't matter now."

"If you keep running I'll keep tracking you down," I told him. "That's the way it has to be. Much easier to give up and come with me today."

He got to his feet and stretched a little. Then he took off like he'd been shot out of a gun. He was a mile away before I could get to my feet. The boy sure could run. I spent a few minutes poking around in his tent. He didn't have much. It was hard to see how he survived, but then I remembered that he stole everything he needed. That wouldn't continue into the winter. There'd be no one to steal from unless he switched to vacant cabins as the Beech Mountain Hermit had done. Hunger can drive a person to most anything I suppose.

I came back later that night, but he didn't return. I made myself comfortable in the bushes and waited. I was there most of the next day. I gave up and went back to my camp to get some nourishment and proper rest. When I returned to Pennington's, it was still vacant. I checked his tent, but nothing was missing. He had spent two nights away from the place. I hope he hadn't abandoned it. I spent the day trout fishing in the creek. It took me a while, but I landed a decent sized rainbow for dinner. The fish was roasted over the fire and tasted pretty good considering I had no seasoning or side dishes. It was the first mountain trout I'd eaten. Fishing had become sport rather than sustenance since I moved here. During my days in Florida, not catching a fish meant not eating sometimes. How things had changed.

I snuck back to check on Pennington that night, but everything was gone. He'd packed up and moved on, probably far away. This ordeal was going to drag on for far too long. I went back to my tent and consulted the map. I'd already covered the majority of the Chatham Wildlife area, so I guessed that he'd try to hide on the other side of Lovelace Creek. Stone Mountain State Park was on the far eastern side of the bush. He wouldn't get too close to that, but close enough to rob campsites. I'd have to relocate my camp again, that meant packing and hiking with a load. It also meant crossing the creek.

It took me most of the day to break down and then find a way to the other side of the creek. I performed a delicate balancing act stepping rock to rock with my pack on. Eventually, I had to get my feet wet, but I made it across. I hiked with wet shoes part way up a slope until I found a level place to pitch the tent and settle in for the night. I had to settle for a granola bar and water dinner. It was too late to go back down to the creek and try to catch a fish. I scanned the map and discovered that multiple smaller creeks ran through the woods in the area. Scott Ridge was between Garden Creek and Widows Creek. It looked like a good place to start searching. I took off my wet socks and hung them up to dry. Pennington wasn't going to make it easy for me.

I reconnoitered the ridge the next day. I didn't find my man, but I did see a few good fishing holes. I had a nice fish dinner that night, which helped to recharge my batteries. I crossed over the ridge the next day and started looking near Widows Creek. Back and forth I went, up and down the slope. Where the hell had he gone? I followed the creek to a waterfall, which was too close to a road for my boy to be hiding. The following day I walked along Bullhead Creek, heading north. I came to a fork in the river, crossed over, and followed Rich Mountain Creek even farther north. I wandered too far from my tent and had to spend a night with no shelter and no food. I did not find Pennington, but I could feel him out there somewhere. I was getting close, but I had to retreat the next morning and get back to my camp. I ate the last of my food stores. I was down to just a few bottles of water. I had to decide to keep up the hunt or call for a pickup. I knew in my bones that I was close, but I also knew that I'd soon be hungry and thirsty. I chose to move my base over to Rich Mountain Creek and try to catch fish. There was a trailhead near Stone Mountain Road where Brody could pick me up, but first I'd give it one more try.

A successful fishing trip led to a decent dinner. It would keep me going for another day. A full belly led to a good night's sleep, and I was ready to hike in the morning. I moved quickly until I could pick up where I left off. I slowed down and went silent as I took a river fork to follow Bullhead Creek.

There was a housing development to the east, and I didn't think Pennington would be there. Eventually, I turned back west towards Garden Creek and Devils Garden. My senses began to pick up on human activity where there shouldn't have been any. I went into super stealth mode and snuck carefully through the brush until I could see the tattered tent that Pennington used. I did not approach him. Instead, I settled in and observed. I'd been out of contact with him for days, so he probably thought he was in the clear.

He'd made camp quite deep in the wilderness. It was a good hike to the nearest campground or the state park. Only by stubborn determination had I found him. Now I had to decide what to do about it. I had no more food and was down to my last bottle of water. If I spooked him, there would be no more following him. I'd have to give up and go home. I made a waypoint on the GPS and slithered away from his camp. I knew where to find him. I needed to regroup before trying to reason with him again. Once I was well clear of the area, I picked up the pace and made my way to the trail that led back out of the woods to Longbottom Road. I dug the phone out of my pack and turned it on. I had enough signal to call Brody.

"There's a park service road by the Little Stone Mountain Baptist Church," I told her. "I'll be coming out there."

"On my way," she said. "You okay?"

"All good," I said. "Tired and hungry."

"Okay, be safe."

The hike out of there became drudgery. I was no longer on the hunt. I had no goal to accomplish but to get home to a hot shower and a warm bed. I don't know how young Pennington did it day in and day out for so many months. He must sneak into camp showers occasionally. I kept putting one foot in front of the other until I made the service road. It was easy walking from there. Brody was waiting when I got out close to the road. Seeing her warmed my heart, and made me question why I'd ever leave her for so long, especially to sleep out in the woods.

"What's the verdict?" she asked as I got in the car.

"I'm on him," I said. "But I'm out of everything. He'll keep."

"So, you're coming back here again?"

"I talked to him a couple of times," I said. "He moved his camp, and I found him again. Then I lost him for a while, but now I know where he is."

"How are you going to bring him in if he keeps running?"

"I've got an idea," I said. "But first, get me something to eat and take me home."

We stopped at Five Guys in Boone on the way home. Normally I hate fast food, but I woofed down a pretty good burger. I could have eaten half a cow, but I couldn't wait for a sit-down restaurant to cook me a steak. I hit the shower as soon as we got to the cabin. I had an urge for a glass of whiskey afterward, but I resisted. I paid some attention to Red before it got dark. I had planned to pay some attention to Brody before bed, but I fell asleep on the couch. She put a blanket over me and let me sleep, knowing that I needed it.

I made up for it in the morning, even before coffee. I was rewarded with a good old fashioned country breakfast of sausage gravy and biscuits. It was good to be home. Pennington could eat his stolen cold cuts and sleep on the ground, but I didn't have to. All I had to do was figure out a way to get him out of there without having to spend the night in the woods again. This consumed my thoughts for the next few days.

Brody presented me with a backlog of potential customers for Creekside Investigations.

"If we keep ignoring the calls we'll be out of business," she said. "We need to start chopping away at this list."

"I'm close to ending this with the running man," I said. "I think I can bring him home."

"How?"

"I use Red to distract him," I said. "He loves animals. He won't be able to resist old Red. As soon as he lets his guard down, I nab him."

"You can't hurt him," she said.

"I was thinking of handcuffs," I said. "However I can use them. Cuff us together, cuff his feet, whatever works."

"What if he gets away before you can restrain him?"

"Then me and Red meet you back at the trailhead," I said. "But that will be my last shot at him. He won't trust me again if I fail."

"What if I come with you?" she asked. "I can carry cuffs too. Double our chances."

"You sure you want to do that?"

"Can't let you and Red have all the fun," she said. "You know where he is. I don't have to slink all through the wilderness. We let Red approach him and hope he stays still long enough for one of us to grab him."

"Sounds like a plan."

# SEVENTEEN

We did not pack for a long stay. We took enough water for the two of us with a little extra for Red. We had the GPS, handcuffs borrowed from Rominger, and our weapons. Traveling light allowed us to move faster. We made a beeline for Pennington's location, allowing Red to run freely. We stopped to catch our breath and drink before we got too close. Red was happy to be out in the woods again. He lived for this stuff. I think he even knew that he was part of a mission. He didn't chase after squirrels or even wander far from our side.

We moved a little slower after that, sneaking up on Pennington's camp. I kept Red on a short leash until we were within striking distance. I whispered to him as I took the leash off.

"Go in there and play nice, boy," I said. "Make nice with him. It's okay, go ahead."

He cocked his head sideways as I spoke, trying to understand. I gave him a little pat on the rump.

"Go play," I said. "Go on, now."

He trotted off in front of us, and we followed carefully, making sure we weren't seen. Red found the camp and ambled in, sniffing everything in sight. The running man came out of his tent and smiled.

"What are you doing here?" he said to the dog. "Are you a good boy?"

Red went right for him. Pennington was still on his knees as the dog approached him. Red gave him a big wet doggy kiss right on the face, which made his smile grow even bigger. He reached out to pet Red, who sat down and let the petting commence.

"You're such a pretty dog," Pennington said. "We need to find your owner. Where did you come from?"

Red gave him another lick, which caused him to giggle like a child. Soon the two of them were rolling around on the ground, alternately wrestling and hugging. I looked at Brody and gave her a nod. It was time to move in.


Pennington was oblivious to our presence. He was having a grand old time playing with Red. He didn't spot us until we were almost on top of him. He froze when he saw us, but didn't run.

"That's our dog," I said. "He likes you. It's okay, you can play with him."

"You sure it's okay?" he asked.

"He loves attention," I said. "He'll keep that up all day."

"Why did you bring him here?"

"To meet you," I said. "I thought you two might hit it off."

"Mom never let me have a dog," he said. "She said I wouldn't take care of one."

"I bet you'd take great care of a dog," Brody said. "And Red does seem to like you."

"And I like him," he said. "I love animals, and they love me. It's a gift, you know."

"Clearly," Brody said. "Do you mind if we sit for a while?"

"Long as I can keep playing with Red," he said.

We got comfortable while Pennington tossed a stick for Red to fetch. I knew that this could go on for hours. Red would retrieve it as many times as it was thrown.

"He ain't Red," Pennington said. "Why'd you name him that?"

"It's after a dog in a country song," I said. "Red was the warden's dog who thought chasing escaped prisoners was fun, but a pretty little female hound dog ruined his career. They had red headed, blue tick puppies."

"I heard that song," he said. "I ain't no escaped prisoner though."

"You sure can run," I said.

"I've always been a runner," he said. "That's my thing."

"I bet the coach could use you to help with the team," I said.

"Coach never liked me much."

"That's not what he told me," I said.

"What did he tell you?"

"Said he had a soft spot for you," I said. "Wanted us to make sure you were all right."

"You talked to my mom, too?"

"I've spoken with her several times," Brody said. "She loves you and wants you to come home."

"Ain't folks mad that I've been stealing stuff?"

"That's no way to live," I said. "You'll get in real trouble sooner or later if you keep it up."

"It will be winter soon," Brody added. "There won't be campers out here then. You'll need a warm place to sleep and some of mom's cooking."

"What are you going to do when it gets cold?" I asked.

He kept throwing the stick, and Red kept bringing it back, eager for more. Pennington seemed delighted each time the stick returned. After it was dropped at his feet, he'd rub Red's head and throw it again.

"I thought I could get into one of those cabins across the road from the park," he said.

"That will get you caught for sure," I said. "Plus they don't leave the heat on when no one is around. There's no food or clothes there when they aren't rented. That's a trap you won't get out of."

"What am I supposed to do then?" he asked. "I like it out here with no people. People ain't nice."

"I'm a pretty nice person," Brody said. "I want to help you."

"What about him?" he asked, pointing at me.

"He can be nice when he wants to," she said. "Red absolutely adores him, so he can't be all bad."

"Dogs know if a person is mean or not," he said. "They can tell."

"We both want to help," she said. "We wouldn't be out here if we didn't."

"You've gone to a lot of trouble," he said. "Why?"

"Your mother and your coach convinced us you were worth it," Brody said. "We think we have some ideas to help you."

"Help me what?"

"Deal with people a little better," she said. "Then, you won't have to live out here forever."

"People don't like me much."

"They don't understand you," she said. "But lots of people are nice, just like us."

"I don't know about that."

"Is your mom nice? Was your coach nice?" Brody asked.

"Momma is just as nice as she can be," he said. "Coach let me do my own thing. He didn't bother me like the rest of them at school. He was okay, I guess."

"Counting us you've got four friends," she said.

"That's more than I've got," I said. "You don't have it so bad."

He thought about that one for a minute. He was holding onto the stick, and Red was getting impatient. He finally threw it and looked straight at me.

"How come you don't have no friends?" he asked.

"I don't like people much either," I said. "But I make out okay in the world. Finding the good ones, like Brody here, makes putting up with the bad ones tolerable."

"She seems real nice," he said.

"She puts up with me and Red," I said. "Treats us real good."

"Will you bring Red to visit me?"

"Red would like that," I said. "He wants to play more than I can handle sometimes."

"I will play with him all day," he said.

"We'll bring him over once in a while," I said. "Maybe talk your mom into letting you get your own dog."

"You would do that?"

"Looks like you can handle one to me," I said. "I'll talk to her about it if you'll come out of the woods with us."

He stopped throwing the stick. Red plopped down at his feet, panting but happy. He rubbed Red's fur softly, thinking. He looked like a little boy, lost in his thoughts. I couldn't predict what he would decide. I looked at Brody. She had her fingers crossed. Nothing was said for five minutes. He stood up and threw the stick one more time.

"All right," he said. "I'll go home with you, but you better keep your promises."

"Your mother will be so happy," Brody said.

"You made a good choice," I said. "You won't want to be out here this winter."

"I get to play with your dog, right?"

"Sure man," I said. "Let's get you out of here."

Pennington and Red played fetch all the way back to the trailhead. My dog was going to sleep well that night. We carried only a few things from his camp, leaving the tent to rot in the woods. He needed a shower and some clean clothes badly, but we figured his mother wouldn't mind. He didn't talk during the drive to her house. When we got out of the car, he stayed seated. I could see the reluctance on his face. I stayed with him while Brody went to get his mother.

"You're going to be fine," I told him. "Trust me, I know the world can be overwhelming at times, but you can do this."

"It's a lot different than the woods," he said.

"I like the woods too," I said. "Sometimes I go out in the wilderness just to get away from people. I need to get away from all the noise."

"But you always go home," he said.

"I like Brody too," I said. "And a warm bed. We're not meant to stay in the woods forever."

"I kind of knew that," he said. "But I had to get away."

"I understand," I said. "You call me when you get the urge to get away. We can go out in the woods together."

He gave me a smile. His mother came out of the house with an even bigger smile. He got out of the car, and she gave him a monstrous hug.

"I'm sorry, momma," he said. "I didn't want to cause you no trouble."

"Welcome home," she said. "Let's get you cleaned up and fed."

"That would be nice."

She turned to us with tears running down her cheeks. Brody gave her a hug.

"Thank you is not enough," she said. "You're angels, both of you."

I handed her a business card, and she pulled me in for a hug too.

"We promised to bring the dog over for visits," I said. "Give us a call when it's okay."

"I will," she said. "He loves dogs."

"Please consider letting him get one of his own," I said. "That was part of our deal."

"I'll think it over," she said. "God bless you."

Ed Pennington had already gone inside. Mrs. Pennington turned and ran after him, leaving us alone on the sidewalk. Our mission was complete.

# EIGHTEEN

We kept our end of the bargain, taking Red to see young Pennington every few weeks. Brody arranged for a counselor to help him better deal with society. He went to his sessions willingly. I talked to his old coach, who agreed to let Ed run with the team and to call him his assistant. Brody was proud of me for going the extra mile for a complete stranger. I think maybe it was a form of therapy for me. It was certainly out of character. Maybe I wasn't too old to learn new tricks.

One day I was alone with Ed, and I took the opportunity to ask him a question.

"All that time you spent out in the wilderness," I said. "Did you ever see any little people?"

"Little people?"

"Real white skin with big eyes," I said. "Maybe three or four feet tall."

"I'm a little slow sometimes," he said. "But I ain't crazy."

"So, no little people?"

"Not that I saw."

We returned to work on behalf of suspicious spouses, which was easier but less rewarding. Our clientele continued to be almost exclusively women. Roughly half of them were right about their husband's behavior. Not all the wives whose husbands were deemed innocent seemed happy about our findings, but they all paid the bill.

Local police departments had little use for our skills for the rest of that summer. There were no lost children to find. The meth cookers kept a low profile or moved out of the area. No inmates escaped from prison. The only tracking I did was done in the car, following men who were meeting their mistresses. Our area of operation expanded as word spread. Money was rolling in, but the cheating spouse industry left me with a hollow feeling.

I didn't get a kick out of putting the final nail in the coffin of a failing marriage. I didn't have much respect for the women who were wrong about their husbands either. Relationships can be damn tough. I was no expert, but these people were plain dysfunctional. I learned that I was naïve to the ways of the modern world in that regard. Brody had seen it all before. Our work didn't seem to bother her, so I soldiered on.

Red began to look forward to his trips to West Jefferson to play with Ed Pennington. The two of them would run around the yard and wrestle on the ground for hours. Brody would sit with Mrs. Pennington and chat. The coach had reported that Ed was doing well with his team, even helping some of the boys when needed, not just running along with them. On one of our visits, she confided that she was probably going to let her son get his own dog. We let her know that none of the campers had pressed charges over lost food or damaged tents. The county Sheriff felt no need to pursue charges either, now that the looting had stopped.

We discussed setting a wedding date. The decision was made to do the deed the following spring when the azaleas and rhododendrons were in full bloom. We even booked a date with a popular local venue just outside of Banner Elk. I purchased a ring, and offered it to my future bride one fine summer evening out on the porch, overlooking the creek. We held each other in a long embrace. Brody had tears in her eyes as we separated. She was never more beautiful in my eyes. We celebrated with an expensive stay on Topsail Island. The sand and the sea made me a bit nostalgic for my previous life, but the experience refreshed me before our return to the mountains.

Brody was headed out to the porch one day when the shooting began. The glass in the door shattered and she went down. Our attacker was down by the creek, spraying automatic weapons fire into the cabin. When I got to her, I found a hole in her chest that was sucking air. I knew that to be very bad. I ripped off my shirt and wadded it up over the wound. The shooting stopped, and I heard the man running up the hill towards the back of the house, his boots crunching on the gravel driveway. I put Brody's hand on the shirt and pressed it down.

"Hold this tight," I said.

Her eyes were far away, but she was still breathing.

"Know how much I love you," I said, kissing her on the forehead.

If I stayed there with her, I'd be dead within a few minutes. My survival instinct took over. I grabbed a pistol out of the bedroom and scrambled up the stairs to the loft. Bullets blasted through the glass in the back door, which was at ground level. I got down on the floor and pointed my weapon between the wooden rail banisters, waiting for the shooter to appear. Red woke from his nap and trotted to the kitchen to see what was going on. If I called him, I'd give away my position. I heard the back door open, and Red started growling at the intruder. He was shot down instantly.

Everything that I loved was being taken from me right before my eyes. I'd felt fear before, and somehow always managed to keep my cool. The fear fought with my rage over what I had witnessed. I tried desperately to remain calm, and keep my aim steady. I saw the barrel of a rifle first, and then the shooter himself. I maintained a steady aim as I pulled off five shots, directed at the man's chest. He dropped to the floor, his weapon clattering on the hardwood. I stayed where I was, watching his body for a minute. I was prepared to fire again at the slightest twitch. He was less than twenty feet away, and all my rounds had hit him.

Finally, I climbed down, keeping an eye on him. I gave a quick glance at Brody and didn't like what I saw. Red's blood was pooling on the kitchen floor. I stood over the man, pointing my gun at him. Then I saw the vest. Did my bullets penetrate it? He opened his eyes and looked up at me. I shot him in the forehead. He would never look at anything again. I didn't know who he was, and I didn't care. I only cared that he was dead.

Brody was gone by the time I returned to her. I worked on her like an army field medic, but it was fruitless. I prayed for a miracle, but it didn't come. I cursed the very God that I had just prayed to. I sat on the floor with my head in my hands, trying to comprehend what had just happened. I couldn't think. I knew that I needed to call the police, though. Instead of dialing 911, I called Rominger.

"Shooter came to the house," I told him. "He killed Brody. I killed him. Red's dead too. Send in the troops, but there's no hurry. No one left alive but me."

"Jesus Christ, Breeze," he said. "Are you hurt? Do you need an ambulance?"

"Hurts like hell, man," I said. "But not from bullets. Just get here as fast as you can."

"On my way," he said. "Hang in there."

I threw my phone through the open back door into the driveway. I picked up Brody's phone and took it outside too. I proceeded to smash them both into tiny bits. I carried our computer out back and shot it until I was out of bullets. I went back to Brody and sat with her until the first cop car showed up. An officer I didn't know came in with his weapon drawn. I put my hands up.

"I'm not armed," I said. "My weapon is there on the counter. It's empty."

He holstered his gun and took a look around.

"You Breeze?" he asked. "Are you hurt?"

"I'm not wounded," I said. "Can I get up?"

"Try not to touch anything," he said. "We'll get the detectives up here shortly."

"I'm going to go outside," I announced.

"You're going to have to sit in my car until we get some more people on scene," he said. "Sorry, procedure."

He led me by the arm to the back seat of his patrol car. He shut the door after I sat down. I knew I couldn't open that door, and it gave me claustrophobia. I started to sweat, and I couldn't unclench my teeth. Both of my fists were balled up as tight as they could get. I tried to loosen them, but they kept closing tight again. Rominger arrived and rescued me. I walked him through the scene and explained how it all went down. He wouldn't let me move Brody or Red until the detectives got a look.

They showed up and asked a hundred questions and took a hundred pictures. The only question I couldn't answer was who the guy was. Rominger and I told them about my beef with Cody Banner, and how I had killed him. We also discussed the former Banner Elk Police Chief. The shooter could have been a friend or relative of either. I knew but didn't discuss the fact that he could have come from Florida, or been hired by someone from my past. Either way, my location was known. I'd never be safe here. I knew I was going to have to leave.

One of them tilted the shooter on his side. The back of his skull had been blown to bits. There was a jagged hole in the floorboard where my .40 caliber bullet had lodged. They extracted it and placed it in an evidence bag. An ambulance pulled up, and his body was hauled out. I lifted Red from the floor and carried him to the back yard. A second ambulance came for Brody. I stood in the driveway trembling as they wheeled her out. I stopped them and went to her side. I pulled the sheet down from her face, kissing her one last time.

"I'm sorry, baby," I whispered to her. "I'm so sorry."

They loaded her in the ambulance and drove away. Rominger stood in front of me with his head down.

"I don't know what to say, brother," he said. "You can come stay at our place if you want."

"I don't think so," I said. "I've got a lot of work to do here."

"I can get a crew here to clean up," he said.

"That would be great," I said. "Not sure I can do it."

"I'm on it," he said. "Anything else you need, just ask."

He pulled out his phone to make a call. I went to the garage and got a shovel. I worked at digging a hole for Red for an hour. I hit solid rock three feet down. I got his favorite blanket and wrapped him up before gently placing him in the hole. After he was covered, I carried rocks from the edge of the creek and covered his grave. I couldn't have any predators digging him up. I worked like a soulless robot, trying not to replay the day's events in my mind. The cleaning crew arrived, and I showed them what they needed to do.

My closest neighbor came by to find out what had happened. We'd purchased the cabin from him. He was the one who'd built it. He offered to get the windows replaced the next day. I accepted.

"What are you going to do?" he asked.

"I don't know," I said. "You want to buy a cabin?"

"We could probably come to some agreement," he said.

"I'll let you know."

Eventually, everyone left and I was alone. I had orders not to leave town, but no one was keeping tabs on me. The blood and gore had been erased, and the broken glass had been swept up. Thin plastic had been taped where glass used to be. It was deadly quiet, except for the ever-present hum of the creek. I stood in the middle of the cabin and let the tears come. The complete realization that Brody was gone forever hit me so hard that I thought I'd collapse. In one day, it had all come to an end. Life in the mountains had turned on us in an instant, leaving nothing but death.

Suddenly I hated that cabin. There was nothing left in it for me. I couldn't stay there that night. I grabbed some water and left, passing by Red's grave and up the hill to the woods. I walked long and hard until I reached the plateau. I watched the sun go down over Banner Elk, completely alone in the world. I spent the night in Pop's cave, lying in the dark mourning my loss. No image of the old man came to offer me wisdom. I had no dreams that gave me hope. I'd never been more alone.

# NINETEEN

In the morning I hiked quickly back down the mountain. I went to the neighbor's place with my bank account information in hand. He offered me something less than what I had paid for the cabin, but I didn't care. I took it and asked him to wire the money to my account. He said the glass company would be there later in the day. I suggested that the bill would be his, as it would soon be his house. He produced a power of attorney which I signed.

I drove into town and stopped in the local funeral home. It was Brody's desire to be cremated. She wanted her ashes poured over a waterfall that was close to our home. It was her favorite spot in the mountains. We'd been there several times in the course of our missions, but she liked to return on our free time. She would just sit and watch. It was a peaceful place.

"Can you or someone take her ashes there and fulfill her final wishes?" I asked.

"That's generally left up to the family," he said.

"She didn't have any family, except me, and I can't stick around," I said. "I've got my reasons. I'll give you five hundred extra to make sure it's done right."

"I'm sure something can be arranged."

I went back to the cabin and started packing. The first thing I did was round up all of our weapons and put them in the car. The second thing I collected was all of the cash that we had stashed in various hidey holes throughout the house. I put it in a pillowcase and stuffed it into my backpack. I put some clothes and toiletries in a separate bag. I still had room in the car, but there was nothing else I wanted or needed.

I walked through the cabin one last time, swatting away memories that threatened to make me cry again. As I looked out over the creek, I remembered my fishing rod. I found it and added it to the small load in the car. Before getting into the driver's seat, I stood in the driveway and took one last look around.

*Adios, High Country. Breeze is in the wind.*

# Author's Thoughts

I posted a poll on Facebook concerning the future of Breeze. 75% of respondents voted for him to return to Florida to live on a boat. I couldn't rationalize Brody accepting that. Many of you will be disappointed in her death, but it was time for our hero to return to his roots. I hope you will follow along as our hero regains his original grittiness and becomes more removed from the everyday events of modern society. RIP Brody and Red.

Ed Pennington and Jessie Lynn were named after readers who asked to be a character in one of my books. Both characters are completely fictional. If you would like for me to use your name in a future book, feel free to contact me at kimandedrobinson@gmail.com.

I'd love to grow my email list. It will be used to announce new releases and special offers. Sign up at the following link:

https://mailchi.mp/6ca0c23d88dc/signup

*If you liked this book, please leave a review at Amazon. Reviews are greatly appreciated.

You may also wish to "Like" my author page on Facebook to keep up with the latest.

https://www.facebook.com/EdRobinsonAuthor/

The Brown Mountain Lights are a real phenomenon. They've been seen hundreds of times over the years but there is still no scientific consensus as to what causes them.

There really is a statue of the Moon-eyed People in the Cherokee North Carolina History Museum.

# OTHER BOOKS IN THE MOUNTAIN BREEZE SERIES

Banner Elk Breeze
https://amzn.to/2JsvpdM

Blue Ridge Breeze
https://amzn.to/2WaxQHz

Beech Mountain Breeze
https://amzn.to/2LWg1YY

High Country Breeze
https://amzn.to/2HDH45T

# TRAWLER TRASH SERIES

Trawler Trash; Confessions of a Boat Bum
https://amzn.to/2JqXFNJ

Following Breeze
https://amzn.to/2JNjM0k

Free Breeze
https://amzn.to/2LQZQMD

Redeeming Breeze
https://amzn.to/2JPmLVO

Bahama Breeze
https://amzn.to/2JusIbl

Cool Breeze
https://amzn.to/2VBo0dI

True Breeze
https://amzn.to/2JQHUyT

Ominous Breeze
https://amzn.to/2EhHzSu

Restless Breeze
https://amzn.to/2w9P5Ks

Enduring Breeze
https://amzn.to/2HHktW6

Benevolent Breeze
https://amzn.to/2VPXSR9

# NON-FICTION BOOKS
## BY ED ROBINSON

Leap of Faith; Quit Your Job and Live on a Boat
https://amzn.to/2LUK4QR

Poop, Booze, and Bikinis
https://amzn.to/2HEWHKz

The Untold Story of Kim
https://amzn.to/30saPiP

# ACKNOWLEDGEMENTS

**Proofreaders:**

Jeanene Olson

Dave Calhoun

Laura Spink

**Editor:**

John Corbin

**Cover Design:**

https://ebooklaunch.com/

**Interior Formatting:**

https://ebooklaunch.com/

Made in the USA
Middletown, DE
26 September 2020

20597233R00179